Teapot Tales

a collection of unique fairy tales

Copyright Melusine Muse Press© 2013
Property of the Chapter Book Challenge

www.MelusineMusePress.com

This is dedicated to all of the members of the Chapter Book Challenge and everyone who loves creating magic through storytelling.

Table of Contents

Elf Dance *by C. S. Frye* 6
Hansel and Gretel *by Kelly McDonald* 9
Tears of the Dark Fairy *by Rebecca Fyfe* 11
Rosebloom and Brujaja the Ogre *by Brenda A. Harris* 14
The Frog Prince *by Melissa Gijsbers* 17
Forever After *by Jackie Castle* 19
The Frog Princess *by Nicole Zoltack* 21
Snow White and the Pirates *by Ashley Howland* 23
Stone Hearts *by Melinda E. Lancaster* 25
Puss in Boots *by Bron Rauk-Mitchell* 27
The Legend of Just So *by Satori Cmaylo* 30
The Tortoise and the Little Bird *by Elizabeth Gallagher* 33
Rooblefound *by Linda Schueler* 35
Fighting Dragons *by Robert Fyfe* 38
Crimson *by Julia Lela Stilchen* 41
Before *by Tia Mushka* 44
Prince Peter *by Cecilia Clark* 45
Will the Stars Still Shine? *by Theresa Nielsen* 48
Tom Thumb in Hot Water *by Yvonne Mes* 50
Jack and the Giant *by David Jamieson* 53

Fairy Fractures *by Angelica Fyfe* 55

Lise & Nat *by Rebecca Fyfe* 56

Rapunzel *by Melissa Gijsbers* 58

Midnight's Tale *by Brenda A. Harris* 60

Toadly Awesome *by C. S. Frye* 63

Dicky and the Dragon *by Elizabeth Gallagher* 65

Spring Folly *by Jackie Castle* 68

The Sacred Scepter *by Nicole Zoltack* 70

The Three Little Cherry Trees *by Linda Schueler* 73

A Name and a Wish *by Ashley Howland* 75

Cindy and Ella *by Cecilia Clark* 78

The Raven Girl *by Rebecca Fyfe* 80

The Princess and the Pea *by Melissa Gijsbers* 82

How Shadow Saved His Fairy *by Brenda A. Harris* 84

Faery Pond *by C. S. Frye* 87

About the Authors 90

The Chapter Book Challenge 97

Elf Dance

by C. S. Frye

The breeze whipped the tassels on Dala's skirt. She swallowed, awaiting her turn in the contest. She adjusted her ankle brace. What if she missed a step? Then she would never fit in. Her performance must be perfect. She hoped her elf abilities would be enough to keep her in control.

A halo of moonlight shined brightly over the clearing amid the trees. She focused with all her heart and leaped into the air. Dala whirled like a leaf in the wind. Her blood raced as she danced above the crowd.

The louder the crowd yelled, the faster she danced. Her body fell and rose with an internal song—the music of Elves. The crowd jumped up and down in a frenzy.

Last night, she had dreamed she won the contest. The dream was obviously an omen.

The light caressed her every footstep. It glowed upon her skin and followed every wave of her slender arms; enfolding, circling, enhancing each step of her well-trained feet. Her stomach tightened, daring to push herself to dance better than ever before. She twirled with confidence, leaped with determination with all the flair of a true elf.

Dala's body glittered in the sunlight. She could dance all night but the thrill of it vanished when her performance ended. The crowd hushed as she performed the final steps. She gently floated down, twirling to the center with the ease of a quill in the breeze.

Her ankle twisted. She stumbled into an awkward tumble. Her heart stopped for an instant. The crowd gasped.

Dala acted quickly, turning the fall into a spin. Then she fell on her knees and slumped forward in a perfect – soundless – bow.

The crowd cheered; "Dala, Dala, Dala!"

The Queen's messenger stepped to the front and unrolled a scroll; "The Queen extends her thanks to everyone for coming to our festival and especially the performers."

The fairies hurried to Dala's side, grabbing at her, hugging her, and squealing with delight.

Dala glanced past the fairies. She fastened loose strands of hair and tried to stop her knees from wobbling.

"Attention, please. This award is for only the most artistic at heart," the Queen's voice echoed over the crowd. "I present it only to those who show extraordinary abilities. Will Selphia step forward?"

Dala's hand trembled as Selphia accepted the trophy.

Cheers roared from the assembly. The roaring rose above the treetops and seemed to never end. Dala wished it might end, for this made three years she had failed.

Dala walked toward the clearing. Her friends gathered around her, chattering and praising her performance. She didn't speak. Why were they congratulating her? Her cheeks warmed.

"You should have won," said Quin. "You danced plume-like . . . like a fairy."

Beads of sweat formed on Dala's brow. "I was awful! I ruined everything! I'm a complete failure!"

"Oh no. You danced exquisitely! Like a true fairy," said Quin. "If it weren't for your ankle, you would have won."

Dala grimaced. She had bungled the routine. And she wasn't a fairy—she was an Elf!

Dala gazed at the fireflies in the treetops. "Next spring. I'll win!"

An arm dropped around her shoulders. Dala turned.

"We're going to the river to cool ourselves, come join us," coaxed Quin.

"I don't feel like swimming. I lost the contest."

"Everyone says you should have won. You were the best dancer, not that sprite, Selphia! Please come . . . everyone wants you to."

Dala swallowed. "Really?"

She let Quin take her hand.

Her tassels fluttered in the breeze as Quin led her toward her friends at the river.

Hansel and Gretel
by Kelly McDonald

The children had been dead for five years. Mavis' wrinkled hand caressed the cold glass of the frame. Gretel's chubby faced smile and Hansel's mischievous grin peered out of the sepia toned picture.

Mavis lips trembled. It was time to pack up what had turned into a shrine for her grandchildren. She wouldn't put away her mourning clothes; her wardrobe only held black garments anyway.

If only her son hadn't married that woman. It was never proven that she was responsible for the loss of the children, but Mavis knew it. Her son hadn't lived out the year, in his grief.

Packing the photos off the mantle, her hand found the forgotten newspaper article folded behind a frame.

The news clipping! It told of the old woman who lived in a cabin not unlike the one Mavis dwelled in. A farmer had called upon the house when his horse had foundered. After knocking, and receiving no answer, he had entered the cabin.

He had cried in horror as inside he found sitting in its own filth, covered in sores, a child locked in a cage. He saw another tethered to a pole, rocking back and forward, eyes vacant, scratching silently at the wall. There was a huge fireplace, burning brightly. When the police were summoned they were distraught to find the remains of human bones inside.

Mavis felt the chill run through her. Had that been the way her grandchildren had died? Had the old woman found and killed her grandbabies?

She startled at a knock upon her door, clutching her heart in fright. The knock was loud and impatient, like the person had already rapped against the frame unheard more than once.

Mavis looked up to see two young men peering in through her window. With news clipping still in hand, she opened the door. Mavis looked at the taller one. He was so much like Hansel would have been, strapping, strong and with the dark hair of his father.

Mavis smiled at the boys. They were looking for work. There wasn't much that Mavis could offer them, but with the memory of her grandson still lingering in her mind, she asked the boys to cut some wood. Winter was coming, and it was a job she didn't enjoy. She was getting too old. The winter of her life seemed to be dragging on, longer than any season should.

The boys took the work gratefully, and went out to the shed.

"Did you see her?" said Johnie.

"I did." Replied Marco, swinging the axe.

"Do you think it is her… the one they have been looking for all these years?"

"I don't."

"But she was almost gloating! She had the clipping of her deed in her hand…you didn't see it?"

"I saw an old lady."

Johnie didn't buy it. His cousin went missing years before. The story of the hagkiller was well known to him. This woman, he knew it was her. Picking up some cut wood, he headed towards the cabin. The woman had gone into the bedroom. Dropping the wood in the box, Johnie peered about. He saw a doll, a dirty old teddy, and a small wooden train. The clipping now lay upon the table. He looked at the fire place. It was the old fashioned kind, big enough to burn a child's body. It was her, he knew it.

He went back out to Marco.

"It's her. She still has souvenirs' in there. I saw the kids' toys! It's her I tell ya."

Marco looked back at the cabin. The old woman was peering at them through the curtained window. She had a smile on her face.

"Jesus Marco, look. It's the Hagkiller."

Without pause, Johnie swung up the axe and headed inside. Mavis was just coming out of her room. She saw the boy striding towards her. Her smile faltered. She saw what he meant to do. The other boy was coming behind him, but Johnie was already swinging. She smiled as she crumpled. Winter had gone, and in the light of spring, she saw the smiles of her grandbabies.

Tears of the Dark Fairy
by Rebecca Fyfe

Isabella's mother had fallen very ill. Her mother had grown deathly pale and listless. She lay in her bed and barely moved. Sometimes, Isabella would put her hand in front of her mother's face just to make sure she was still breathing. The healer woman from her village had not been able to make her mother well. Her father rarely left her mother's bedside anymore. Isabella knew her mother was dying.

Isabella remembered a tale told around the village about a magic cure that could heal any illness. The villagers whispered about the dark fairy queen. She lived in a palace at the top of the mountain that rose up at the northern edge of the village. The dark fairy queen's heart had been encased in ice many years ago, and now she lived alone and felt nothing. No emotions could ever get through the ice around her heart. It was said that the magical cure was contained in the tears of the dark fairy queen. But, as the fairy queen never felt sadness or joy, she never shed any tears.

Isabella loved her mother very much, and she was desperate to find a cure. So one day, she packed a satchel full of some fruit, nuts, bread, a change of clothes and her favorite book and set off to go to the palace to find a way to melt the ice around the dark fairy queen's heart. It was the only way she could save her mother.

After a tiring journey up the mountain path, she arrived at the palace. Seeing no one in the courtyard, she went straight to the large double doors at the entrance and knocked. After several moments had passed, the door was answered. Isabella knew right away that the one who answered the door was the dark fairy queen herself, because the woman who stood in the doorway was very elegant and wore a crown upon her head. Her dress was a deep purple and her eyes were a deep black. Her pupils seemed to swallow up her eyes and reflected Isabella's image back at her.

"What do you want?" asked the dark fairy queen, her face showing no expression at all.

"I seek employment," Isabella said. She knew it would take some time for her to find a way to melt the ice around the fairy queen's heart. She only hoped it would be in time to save her mother.

"What kind of employment?" asked the queen. "What can you do?"

"Well, I can read and write. Perhaps you need a scribe?"

"I have no need for a scribe, but perhaps you can read to me," answered the fairy queen. "My eyes don't see as well anymore and it's difficult to read for myself. I used to love hearing stories spoken out loud, and, as nothing amuses me anymore, maybe hearing stories once again will amuse me."

Isabella was shown to the servant's quarters. As the dark fairy queen had no other servants, preferring to live alone, Isabella had her choice of rooms. Everything in the palace was very dusty and full of cobwebs. Since Isabella was only required to read to the fairy queen at night, she spent the day cleaning the palace.

An idea had formed in Isabella's mind on how she was going to melt the ice around the dark fairy queen's heart. She was going to achieve her task through the stories she told. Everyone knows that a good story makes you feel and experience everything that its characters feel and experience. So Isabella went into the queen's very large library and selected only the best of stories, ones that could not fail to evoke emotions.

Each night, Isabella read three stories to the fairy queen. And, with each story, a tiny bit of emotion would get through the ice of the queen's heart and the ice slowly began to crack. Isabella knew that her mother didn't have much time, so on the third night, for the third book, she pulled her own book out of her satchel, the one she had brought with her. This book had always been her favorite and never failed to bring tears to her eyes when she read it.

As Isabella read the stories to the queen on that third night, more of the ice cracked and melted away from the queen's heart. As Isabella read the third book, her favorite, the ice completely melted around the dark fairy queen's heart and her deep black eyes faded to a soft, warm brown. Tears fell freely down her cheeks, which Isabella quickly scooped up into a tiny bottle she had brought for the purpose of storing the queen's tears.

Isabella told the queen about her mother's illness and the fairy queen went with her to her home and watched as Isabella made her mother drink the tears from the bottle. By the next day, Isabella's mother was healthy again and everyone rejoiced about the fairy queen's newly warmed heart.

Rosebloom and Brujaja the Ogre
by Brenda A. Harris

There once was a boy, who was really a girl named Rosebloom. This is the story of how she became known as Prince DeSunne.

Rosebloom lived in a wicked kingdom ruled by an ogre named Brujaja. Brujaja enjoyed stomping through his kingdom causing mayhem and distress. When the townfolk heard his stomps, they ran into the woods to hide. However, a young girl named Rosebloom was unafraid of the ogre. One day, she went out to greet him.

"Ho- hey there, King Brujaja. Are you out for a pleasant walk this fine morning?"

"A pleasant walk?" said the ogre. He raised his eyebrows in disbelief at such insolence coming from a human.

"Aye, yes," said Rosebloom, "I'm about to go for a walk, too. Want some company?"

"What makes you think you should even be in my presence? I will have you drown for this!" said Brujaja, but Rosebloom just laughed. Her laugh was sweet music to his ears and Brujaja, being an ogre, did not like it. "After you drown, I will have you thrown off a cliff for the vultures to eat."

"Do what you wish," said Rosebloom, "if you can catch me." She ran to the fig tree that grew beside his castle and nimbly climbed up to the top. There, she nibbled on figs and sang, "Do as you wish, if you can catch me, Brujaja. Do as you wish."

This made Brujaja furious. He stomped after her, but could not climb the tree. Rosebloom laughed. She leaped onto the top of the castle wall. There she danced and sang, "Do as you wish Brujaja, if you can catch me. Do as you wish." The ogre charged the wall head on, but the wall did not crumble. Again, Rosebloom laughed. Brujaja roared a frightful roar and tore at his beard. Fuming, he went home.

The next day, Brujaja decreed, "All fruit trees must be chopped down!" The townspeople did as he bid. None dared complain.

On the third day, he decreed "Every singing creature is to be caged and brought to me!" The residents did as he bid. None dared complain.

On the fourth day, Brujaja announced, "All the kingdom girls will be imprisoned in my dungeon forever." The townsfolk cried out for mercy. Brujaja refused to listen. His army of ogres scoured his kingdom destroying home and farm, until every girl was captured and herded to his dungeon. The townspeople, overcome with grief, wept deeply. Brujaja was as happy as an ogre can be, which is not much.

A day came when a prince arrived. He marched to the ogre's castle and stated, "I, Prince DeSunne, would like a visit with his glorious highness, King Brujaja."

When greedy Brujaja heard Prince DeSunne's request, he devised a wicked scheme to trap and hold the prince for ransom. For the ogre thought, surely, the prince's life was worth much gold. Brujaja invited the prince to enter his castle, but Prince DeSunne disdainfully refused.

"In my castle," said Prince DeSunne, "the walls are lined with peasants. It's such joy to hear them say, 'Prince DeSunne rules over us. Long live our prince.' Do you have any such wonder in your castle?"

"No," said Brujaja, "I just have an old castle."

"Of course not," said the prince, pinching his nose. "My kingdom has sapphire rivers, diamonds for stars, and the sun is molten gold. I see none of that here."

"Go on, tell me more."

"I think I've said enough."

 I would like to visit your kingdom," said Brujaja, "Where is it at?"

"Why, everyone knows where my kingdom is."

"I don't," said the ogre, "and I want to see it, now."

"Sure," said the prince. "Just ask any peasant where the Kingdom of DeSunne is. They will point the way."

So, Brujaja and his army set out to find DeSunne's kingdom. The prince was true to his word. Everyone Brujaja asked, "Do you know where the Kingdom of DeSunne is?" sent him on his way with but the point of a finger.

When the ogre left, Prince DeSunne gathered the townsfolk. He ordered them to unlock the dungeon doors and free the prisoners. They did as he bid. Then, the prince removed his disguise, and everyone cheered joyfully for they recognized their sweet Rosebloom.

And so dear reader, if you should meet an ogre who asks you where the Kingdom of DeSunne is, don't be frightened. Just point towards the sun, and he'll be on his way.

The Frog Prince
by Melissa Gijsbers

Clara walked along the path by the lake, glad to get away from her family and the pressure they were putting on her. As the first born, she was the heir and would one day be queen of their tiny kingdom.

"You have to get married," was something she had heard her whole life. "And he has to be a prince."

"The prince of what?" Clara muttered as she kicked a stone.

"Ow!"

"Who said that?" Clara swung around, not seeing anyone there, she walked on.

"You hit me in the head with a rock, and then walk away?"

Clara spun, the path was empty.

"Show yourself," She called out. Hearing a splash on the lake, she went closer.

"Here I am." She saw a frog on a lily pad, rubbing his head and holding a simple gold crown in one flipper. "Where's my apology?"

"I'm sorry. I didn't mean to hit you in the head with that stone." Clara knelt down for a closer look. Other than the crown, the frog was just an ordinary frog. "Are you a prince?"

"Yep," the frog put the crown on his head, careful to avoid the sore spot where the stone had hit him. "Prince Rupert, prince of the frogs of Glass Lake, at your service Princess." The frog bowed awkwardly, holding his crown in place so it wouldn't fall into the lake again.

Clara thought for a minute. "Would you be able to help me with something?"

"If it's within my power." The frog leapt onto the shore and landed on Clara's lap.

Clara bent over and whispered in the frog's ear. The frog laughed. "Wonderful," he clapped his flippers together, "When do we start?"

"No time like the present," Clara grinned and stood up with the frog in her hand. She ran up the path toward the castle.

The banquet was in full swing as Clara descended the stairs. Her hair had been pulled and curled and pinned until her head hurt. The corset in her gown was pulled too tight and she could barely breathe.

"You look beautiful darling." The king met Clara at the bottom of the stairs, ready to present her to the waiting crowd. "Is your prince nearby? I haven't met him yet."

Clara smoothed the skirt of her gown that threatened to trip her with every step. "Yes, he's very close." She smiled a secret smile.

"Ladies and gentlemen," the king called the crowd to attention when they had mounted the dais. "It is with great pleasure for me to announce that my beloved daughter, Princess Clara, is engaged to Prince Rupert." The room erupted in applause. The king looked around. "He's around here somewhere. Prince Rupert, please come and join us."

The frog made his way from his hiding place in the pocket in Clara's gown and jumped on the table in front of the king.

"Your majesty." The frog bowed, one flipper holding on to the crown on his head. "Prince Rupert, at your service."

The queen screamed and fainted, the king stood there, not sure how to react. Clara just smiled.

The king finally found his voice, "Clara, are you out of your mind?" he bellowed.

"You said I had to marry a prince," Princess Clara replied, "You never said what sort."

Forever After
by Jackie Castle

They first met when her parents brought her into his woods as a toddling youngster with wobbling steps. She loved playing in his shade. Over time, her legs grew stronger, her daring bolder. Youthful hands clung to his trunk as she swung like the squirrels also inhabiting his boughs.

Beneath the blazing sun, she hid high in his branches from the demands of home. She delighted in his autumn brilliance and collected his rich acorns by light of the harvest moon. In the winter, he dropped extra limbs for her to collect to make a fire and keep her warm. His spring flowers always adorned her silky black hair.

He grew taller, fuller through the seasons, and his heart loved her more and more. She also grew taller and fuller with time, yet her heart held misty longings – dreams she yearned to realize. Often her yearnings turned to tears he would soak into his bark.

Eventually, her visits were fewer and far between. The tree grew disheartened, even when the forest Dryads came to tend his blossoms in the spring. Despite their enchantments and care, his limbs drooped in loneliness and his leaves browned sooner than the other trees.

One observant Dryad commented on his condition. "Dear tree, your roots go deep and your branches touch the sky but your heart no longer beats with new growth. Pray tell me what troubles you."

The tree roused himself enough to answer. "I once had a friend, so dear to me. She played amongst my branches. I helped her stay warm in the winter and cool in the summer. I even soaked in her tears when she wept. Now, fair Dryad, she's abandoned me and I do not understand what I've done wrong."

"Oh, you have not erred stout one. Such is the way of human hearts. Her life has taken her to new places."

The tree shuddered. His branches, as dried as his broken heart, began to fall around his trunk. The Dryad, couldn't stand to watch the demise of such a wondrous creation. "You are still loved, dear tree. The birds nest in your boughs and feed their young from your fruits. The squirrels enjoy your shade. Do not despair."

"But I miss my laughing friend. I'd give anything to feel her in my branches and watch her hide in my leaves once again."

The Dryad left in frustration. "You're missing out on all the good by letting despair cloud your eyes."

However, the tree didn't listen. Eventually his limbs no longer budded. The birds sought new homes, the squirrels found other playgrounds.

Once again, the Dryad came for her spring visitation. "I see you continue to mourn the loss of your friend."

The tree didn't respond.

"Do you still wish to be close to your young friend, despite how you've been treated, dear tree?"

"I'd give anything to be near her again."

"Well, perhaps your desire will be granted, foolish one."

One winter day, a group of men trudged into the snowy woods with axes. The girl's father was among them. His grayed head bowed, and his voice dripped with the same sorrow the tree felt.

"Here is the oak she once to love to play in," said the father, patting the bared trunk with his hand.

"Perhaps using this one would make her happy," said another man

Hope of seeing his young friend again sent a tingle running down his trunk all the way to his smallest roots. They chopped, cut and sanded. What would he become? A chair? A table? He didn't care. *I said I'd do anything, and I meant it. Whatever it takes to be reunited with her.*

The men fashioned the tree into a narrow, rectangular box. To his relief, he welcomed his friend when they nestled her inside, resting in stillness upon a velvet cushion. And they remained together for all eternity.

Finally, the tree received his wish.

The Frog Princess
by Nicole Zoltack

Prince Jeremy hated being trapped inside the castle walls. Whenever he could, he ducked between the guard's legs and hurried outside to freedom.

One day, he ran and hopped and jumped and raced away until he heard the sound of rushing water. Nearby was a large pond. He cupped his hands and drank the cool water.

"Refreshing, isn't it?"

Prince Jeremy glanced around. No one else was there.

"I'm Princess Marie."

On a large lily pad in the middle of the pond sat an emerald green frog wearing a twinkling crown.

"Did you…can you talk?" Prince Jeremy scratched his head. He never heard of a talking frog before.

"Of course! Why wouldn't I be able to? What's your name?"

"Prince Jeremy." He couldn't believe he was talking to a frog!

Princess Marie hopped onto a rock, then beside him. "Let's play a game."

And so they did. They leapt into the air to see who could jump higher. A tie. Then they swam a lap around the pond. The princess won. Finally, they sang a duet. The prince's voice was definitely not as croaky.

After they were done playing, they sat next to each other beneath a tree near the pond. "How can you talk?" the prince asked.

"A witch cursed me. My father hadn't realized who she was and insulted her."

"That's horrible! Is there no way to break it?"

"A kiss from a prince."

Prince Jeremy wrinkled his noise. The idea of kissing a princess was gross enough but to kiss a frog was even more disgusting!

Still, if he could save her, shouldn't he at least try?

So he cupped her into his hands and kissed her.

Nothing happened.

The prince could tell she was upset as she returned to her lily pad, her crown drooping.

Time passed and at least once a week, the prince journeyed to the pond. They played and talked and developed a friendship. To say goodbye, Prince Jeremy always kissed her. She always remained a frog.

Years went by, and the prince's parents demanded he choose a bride. They brought him lots of princesses to pick from—all beautiful and decidedly human—but he loved none of them. He did not wish to spend the rest of his life with them.

That night, Prince Jeremy made his way back to pond. For the first time, Princess Marie was not on her lily pad.

He sat by the pond and twirled his finger in the water. "Princess Marie, I know you're here. Please come out. I need to talk to you."

She did not appear.

"My parents want me to marry."

No answer. Not even a croak.

"But I don't want to marry anyone."

That wasn't completely true.

"I wish I could break your curse. You're the one I want to marry."

"Prince Jeremy."

He stood and whirled around to see a most stunning princess, the likes of which he had never seen before. But even her beauty could not stir him away from Princess Marie.

"Have you seen a frog?" he asked.

She laughed. "No. But I used to be one."

"Princess Marie?"

She nodded.

Prince Jeremy hugged her and kissed her, and soon they were married, much to his parents' happiness.

Every part of Princess Marie was changed back into human, except for her singing voice. She still croaked, so Prince Jeremy would sing to her, and to the many children they had. And they were all very happy and did their best to not offend anyone, in case they were a witch in disguise.

Snow White and the Pirates
by Ashley Howland

Snow White ran through the forest. She was desperate to get away from the huntsman who had just told her of the Evil Queen's plan. She wiped the tears from her eyes as she ran. The thick branches caught on her dress, ripping it to shreds. Suddenly the ground fell away from underneath her feet. She fell right off a cliff and landed with a thud on the deck of a boat.

Snow White slept for many days. When she awoke there was a man looming over her. He had thick, curly black hair, a bushy moustache and a hook on one hand. The ship bounced over the waves as Snow White tried to sit up. She looked around the room. It was filled with all sorts of treasure. As her head began to clear, she realised the captain was talking.

"What shall we do with you?" he asked.

"Make her walk the plank," said another man, "Women are bad luck to have on ships."

Snow white looked at the second man. His undersized glasses sat uncomfortably on his nose. His red hat was falling off his chubby head. He looked at her like she was some sort of monster.

"Well, what do you have to say for yourself?" asked the captain.

"I know where there is the most amazing treasure," said Snow White, quickly regaining herself.

"Do tell," said the Captain.

Snow White told him of the magic mirror. How it can see the future and find any one. The captain was very interested, but his first mate was still concerned.

"What's in it for you?" he asked.

"You take the mirror and any other treasure, and I get to put an end to the evil Queen," said Snow White.

The ship pulled into the Royal docks in the middle of the night. Snow White and the seven pirates snuck up to the side wall of the castle. Here Snow White led them through a secret passage and through to the treasure room. The pirates began to fill their sacks, while Snow White looked for something. Finally she found the potion that she sought. She bid the pirates fair well and left the room.

"Wait," said the captain, "where is my mirror?"

She gestured for him to follow. They walked up the stair case, to the highest tower. There stood the Evil Queen. She was talking to the mirror.

"Mirror, mirror on the wall, who is the fairest of them all?" asked the Queen.

Snow White quickly jumped out and grabbed the Queen. While they struggled the pirate captain grabbed the mirror. He looked back at Snow White, but decided he had better things to do than to help. He ran back down the stairs with his treasure. Upon reaching the landing he heard a horrible cry from above. His heart began to ache. The captain quickly ran back up the stairs. He was too late.

The Evil Queen stood over a sleeping Snow White, poison dripping from Snow White's mouth. Without thinking the captain dumped the mirror and grabbed the potion from Snow White. He quickly dipped in the end of his hook and stabbed the queen in the heart.

"What have you done?" screeched the Queen as she began to change.

The captain looked at her and replied, "Given you a taste of your own medicine."

"What am I?" asked the Queen as she looked towards the mirror.

The Mirror said, "Now you are the fairest creature in the land."

The Queen stared at herself, she was now a unicorn and all the evil was melting out of her heart.

The captain bent down over Snow White. He gave her a kiss and instantly she awoke.

The pirate captain and his Snow White looked into the mirror.

"Mirror, mirror on the wall, who is the fairest of them all?" they asked.

"Why of course, it's Peter and Wendy," replied the mirror.

The Captain looked at his beautiful bride. Then he smashed the mirror with his hook.

"Let them have it," he laughed.

Stone Hearts
by Melinda E. Lancaster

Once upon a time there was a village upon an island. The men were harsh, treating their women like slaves. The women had soft hearts and loved them anyway. One day, a witch came disguised as a beggar. No one dared to aid her for fear of the consequences. But, one woman's kind heart was saddened at the beggar's decrepit appearance and obvious hunger, and so she bathed the stranger, washed and brushed her hair, and laid a feast before her.

When the men learned that the woman had fed this stranger, they became angry and stoned her to death. The witch then cast off her beggar appearance and cursed the men.

"Ye have hearts of stone, so let it be true. For every act of anger, each blow upon a woman or child, every mistreatment of those less strong, your hearts shall harden, until no blood can flow, and ye shall die."

The men laughed at the beggar witch and threw stones at her, chasing her from the village. The men congratulated themselves, and as they turned, yelling at their women to prepare a feast, each stumbled and grabbed his chest. This angered the men and they beat their women for being slow to prepare their feast. Each blow hardened the men's hearts layer by layer. The men turned ashen as the blood stopped within their veins. Falling to their knees, and with one last gasp for air, each man died with a look of disbelief upon his face, not one hour after being cursed.

The women sent their mourning song to Heaven, and their men upon the sea, in boats laden with flowers. The sons sent arrows of flames into the air, the daughters clung to their mothers' skirts and cried, while all watched the men sink in fire into the sea.

Soon, the beach became laden with stone hearts, and each woman searched for the one she felt belonged to her man; she then took it into her hand and flung it back into the sea, as she now realized how poorly she had been treated. Even still, the waves brought each stone heart back. It is said the stone hearts are hoping for forgiveness, but the children of their children's children remember and forever toss them out to sea, to be worn down into sand.

Puss in Boots
by Bron Rauk-Mitchell

Looking back at the last few weeks, Kendra felt as if she had been living in a fairy tale. She was the only child of the local miller; a kindly widower who had fallen ill. Kendra had cared for her father, ran the mill and looked after the house for as long as she could on her own, but she came to realize that the mill would need to be sold, unless she could immediately secure a loan.

Kendra had headed into Town to talk to the local money lenders. Nearing Town, she had come across Puss in Boots. His companion, Prince Charming, was drowning, and Puss needed help to save him. Kendra had quickly assessed the situation and rescued the Prince. From that moment on, things had progressed very quickly, and before she could take a moment's pause, Prince Charming had swooped in, and saved the old Mill. Puss and the Prince became regular visitors to the Mill and, with her father's blessing, Charming had begun to court Kendra.

Prince Charming was all that his name implied: sweet, generous and kind. He was adored by all who knew him, and Kendra had fallen deeply in love with him. It was a joyful day when they married and her father was moved into the Palace with them. Charming hired someone to run the Mill and her father's health had begun to mend.

After the wedding, things began to change. Charming began to spend less time with her, and Puss became her loyal companion. The Prince's charm was fading and the fairy tale began to crumble. Kendra tried to restore the magic, but to no avail. Her Charming was now more of an ogre. She didn't worry her father with her fears though and began to confide in Puss, instead.

Kendra paused in her reflection and realised that she had not seen Puss for a while. Kendra went in search of him, but after finding no sign of him, she headed off to the lower section of the castle. Many doors in this section were locked. The corridors were dank and Kendra noticed that they were heading towards the basement. She paused. Not sure whether to keep going, she steeled her nerve and continued on. Kendra finally found a door that was unlocked. Cautiously opening the door, she found to her surprise that there was a huge cage in this room, and shackled to the wall, was Puss.

A sob of fear escaped from her mouth and Puss opened his eyes. "Kendra," he croaked. "What are you doing here?"

"I could ask the same of you, Puss!" replied Kendra.

"Please, go back before it's too late," he pleaded. Kendra refused to go away and began to look around for the keys to unlock the cage, while Puss told her his story. Charming was an ogre, in the literal sense. His intention had been to eat her but he had changed his mind and decided to keep her around. The more time he spent in the form of the Prince, the more his true nature came out. "He locked me up because I told him he should release you."

"You and your father have to leave," Puss urged but Kendra shook her head.

"We'll have none of that talk, thank you." She finally located the keys and unlocked the cage and Puss's shackles.

"Your Prince cannot be saved. Over time he will no longer be able to shift to any other shape; except his natural state. He is away so often to hunt and to spend time in his true form. He is an ogre and to try to change him is impossible. If you will not flee, you must defeat him." Seeing her lips begin to form a question, he hurried on. "You must get him to change shapes. If he changes shape to a mouse, I can dispose of him and we will all be free."

Kendra released Puss, and he gave her a potion that would lull Charming into a magical half sleep, wherein he would lower his guard, and Kendra could trick him. Puss hid in the dining room, and on Charming's return, Kendra met him with his favorite drink. She ushered him into the dining room. As they made small talk, the quick acting potion made its way into his system.

"I was reading today of a great ogre that used to live in this area," Kendra began, on seeing that the potion was taking effect. "He had the ability to change his form. He could change into an elephant one minute and then to a dog the next. That must be a remarkable gift. But I doubt he could have changed into a much smaller creature, such as a mouse."

The potion had dimmed Charming's senses, and he was quick to rise to the challenge.

"Pah! Easy!" he cried. Full of his own cleverness, he laughed and without much ado, Charming changed into a mouse. As quick as a flash, Puss jumped out from behind Charming's chair, caught him and gobbled him down.

A few days later, Kendra and Puss made plans to seek adventure, while Kendra's father retired from the Miller's life and instead became the gentle sovereign of the land. Did they live happily ever after? Well, that is a story, for another day.

The Legend of Just So
by Satori Cmaylo

Once upon a time in a province in far off Japan, a province so remote there were no daimyo or samurai to tell the people what was right and what was wrong, there lived a very powerful woman called JUST-SO.

Her real name was Lady Masako and her husband who was the daimyo (ruler) of the province was too ill to care for his subjects, so Lady Masako was only too happy to make the decisions in honor of her husband.

If a peasant stole a chicken, the farmer came to this woman for justice.

Masako would hear what each had to say and hand out her ruling with the words,

"Hear me, for what I am about to say is JUST and thus it is SO." The people heard these words uttered so many times by Masako that she came to be called Lady Just So.

The people of the province always obeyed for to go against her judgement was one sure way to death.

Just-So thought she was very fair, but often times her rulings were rigid and lacked any spark of human decency and compassion.

(Let me give you an example.)

One bright sunny morning as Just-So was prepared to go out and collect money from all who worked her farmland (and she loved money), a frightened young girl ran up to her house and threw herself at Just-So's feet. Instead of curiosity and kindness, Just-So scowled at the beautiful girl, for she was interrupting her plans and that was not easily tolerated.

"Get up woman, and stop that snivelling!"

Oh, Lady Just So, hear my humble plea. My father wishes to sell me to Mr. Kenji to settle a gambling debt of his. Mr. Kenji is old and ugly and surely this cannot be right?"

Just then a wagon pulled up with Michiko's (for that was her name) father and Mr. Kenji.

"Ah, insolent daughter, why do you bother such a woman of importance with your petty problems? The great and Glorious Lady So has much more important things to occupy her fine mind. And a debt is a debt and you are my property! I beg your forgiveness, Lady. I shall whip this child before handing her over to Mr Kenji. My daughter Michiko has no right to upset such a woman of honor."

A noticeably puffed up Lady So smiled, but knew she must be fair and give this some thought, so she put her clenched hand under her chin and pretended to be deep in thought for exactly one minute.

Then she turned and entered her home. Of course, they thought she was in meditation as was her usual routine. In truth Lady So was thirsty and went in for a cool drink. Lady So then raised her chin up with her shoulders back and proudly strode outside with a look as though she had been struggling with a grave decision.

"The father owns the daughter and may use her to pay off his debts. She must marry Mr. Kenji. This is Just and it is SO!"

Michiko burst into tears-"But I love another."

"That is not my problem. The ruling is final. It is just and thus is so"

The three drove away with Michiko looking back with a terrified look, at first, and then her eyes turned to stone

"Lady So, when you meet up with our great Buddha, may he give you a future that is Just and thus is SO," Michiko said before they had driven out of earshot.

Lady So's blood turned cold, but only for a moment, for what is this silly nothing of a girl and how could she possibly influence her future? Wasn't she Lady Just-So, the most powerful woman in these parts?

Lady So replied, "In Matters of great importance, as in Life and Death, one's head must rule over the heart."

Lady So lived a long, powerful and peaceful life filled with great wealth and good fortune. She donated money to various charities in the town, not because she cared about the poor and destitute but because she wanted someone to attend her funeral, as Lady So was never blessed with a child. She gave money to the priests for their temples and had many prayers sent when her husband passed on. He had a great many mourners at his funeral. All who lived in the province thought him a great man to live with Lady So for so long.

When Lady So left this earth to journey to Buddha there were many mourners at the grave site. These people just wanted to make sure Lady So was really dead. Then there was great celebration on the day of her funeral.

Lady So met the great Buddha and proclaimed. "Look, oh mighty one, how my people celebrate my life. I am ready to take my rightful place in your heaven."

The Buddha did not speak at first but smiled and gestured to the door which would lead to Lady's So's new future. "Ah yes, Lady So. I have heard much about you from others who have arrived before you and I can say with conviction that your karmic path will be Just."

As Lady So walked through the door the Buddha turned to one of his disciples and sighed. "That was the hardest decision I have ever made. Living in a world without compassion must be Hell. And that WILL be her next life.

The Tortoise and the Little Bird
by Elizabeth Gallagher

In a lush green forest not too far from where you live, there is a silvery stream that winds through the trees and offers cool water to the animals that live there. Tall trees wave their arms at the sun above, and whisper to the gentle winds that wander by. Birds decorate the green branches with nests made of long grass, fluffy white milkweed, twigs, and fallen petals of brightly colored flowers. In one of these nests lives a small blue bird. He is young, full of energy, and he loves to sing. He sings all day long as he flits about the forest, and sings even as he sits in his nest getting ready to greet the moon and pull a soft blanket of sleep over the day.

Below the little bird, in the wet carpet of grass on the forest floor, lives a large tortoise. She is big and round, and is even older than some of the trees. The tortoise has lived in the forest near the edge of the stream all of her long life. She is now enjoying her retirement and lies quietly in the muddy grass listening to the breeze and to the stream bubble by. Her days would be peaceful and sweet without the loud singing of the tiny blue bird.

One bright day, the ancient tortoise could stand it no longer and called to the little bird. She asked him to come down from the treetops to talk with her, which he did immediately. The tortoise told the little bird how his constant singing was very annoying, that he sang too loudly, that he flew around too fast, and that he wasted his days disturbing others. The little bird told the tortoise that he sang the most beautiful songs he could think of to show how much he loved the forest and all the animals, the winding stream, the lush green trees, and the bright yellow sunshine that spread warmth over everything each day. The tortoise insisted that the little blue bird was selfish and not thinking of anyone else while he sang. She decided that he was not going to listen, and so walked slowly back to her nest in the leaves and grass. There she rested in the cool dirt and thought about the little bird. Above her she heard his song, which she admitted to herself would be quite beautiful if it weren't so loud.

Flitting through the treetops above the world, the little bird thought about the tortoise as he sang. He had known the tortoise since he had burst out of his egg, and loved her as you must love your grandmother, but the more he thought about their conversation, the more irritated he got. The little bird knew that he couldn't live without singing and was sure that he shouldn't have to just because of a cranky old tortoise that just sat around all day. He sang even louder than usual, and made up a new song that used every bit of power in his little body. Below him, in her cool dirt nest, the tortoise heard the little bird's new song and buried her head deeper into the leaves.

    The little blue bird sat on a branch, not far above the tortoise, and looked down at her as she buried her head in the leaves. He began to feel a bit guilty that his songs hurt her instead of making her feel the joy of life that he did. He knew how hard the tortoise had worked all her life, how she had taken such good care of all of her many children as well as the other children in the forest, and how old she was now. Perhaps she deserved a rest and shouldn't have to listen to his exuberant songs every minute of each day. The little bird decided to honor the tortoise and stop singing so much, sometimes for days, and the forest didn't seem so wonderful anymore.

    All of the animals began to notice the silence in the forest. They complained to the wise owl, and the owl decided to visit the little blue bird to see what was going on. The little bird told the owl about the tortoise and how bad he was feeling that he made the tortoise so miserable. The owl called a meeting of the forest elders. The elders, after talking for a few days, decided that they respected the tortoise for her age as well as her dedication to her family and the forest, and were proud of the little bird for showing respect to an ancient one. They told both the little bird and the tortoise that the first step to solving a problem is to see the world through the eyes of another, and then they would know what to do.

    The tortoise, since she was very wise and very old, decided that the little blue bird should enjoy his youth and show his love of life. She told the bird to sing all he wanted to, and she would concentrate on the beauty of his songs. The little blue bird, since he was very young, told the tortoise that he respected her right to peaceful days. He told her that he would sing only when the sun was up and would fly to the tops of the trees to sing more quietly. After that, the tortoise rested peacefully and was lulled to sleep by the gentle song of the little blue bird. The little bird was very happy that his song added beauty to the old tortoise's days.

Rooblefound

by Linda Schueler

The duke rubbed his hands over the fire. "I have found a way for us to make our fortune, my Precious."

Precious stopped combing her hair and looked over at her father. "Oh I knew you would. But how?"

He smiled. "The king is looking for a queen. The test is for someone to be able to spin straw into gold."

She tossed her long, dark hair. "But, Father, I can't do that."

"Don't worry, my Precious. I have many friends in the palace. I will sneak in the gold."

The duke took his daughter's hand and they danced around the room.

At the palace, Precious sat in the room, weeping over the mound of straw. How were they supposed to know that she would be put in the tower formerly occupied by Rapunzel? She looked at her hair. If only it was a little bit longer. Okay, a lot.

A voice jolted her. "What's the matter, my dear?"

She looked up, way, way up. "Grandpa?"

"I'm not your grandpa, my dear," the tall man answered. "But I can help you."

"Can you spin this straw into gold?"

"Yes, my dear...for a price."

"Oh yes, anything. Better than the death that I have been promised if I don't spin the straw into gold."

The tall man licked his lips. "I require your first born child."

"Oh, is that all?" She tossed her hair. "Then so be it."

The tall man studied her face for a long time. Then he sat down and started his task.

One year later, Precious was laying on her bed, weeping into her pillow.

"But my Precious, it is not so bad. Now, you are queen." Her father patted her on her back.

"Yes, but now I am pregnant, and my life is over. We were having such fun, the king and I. And now it's all over."

The duke pulled her up. "Ah, but now my Precious, you will be showered with more gifts. And a woman with a child is even more secure. Just make sure you keep the child close to you."

Her eyes narrowed. "I suppose that's true."

The birth was long and trying. "Take it away." She waved her hand at the child when it was finally produced.

"Yes, give the child to me," the tall man said.

Precious bolted upright. "Wait, no, I've changed my mind. I'll keep the child after all."

"You made a deal with me."

"Guards, seize him!"

"It's too late." He turned towards the door.

"No," she wailed, "I need that child."

"Need or want?" He paused. "Okay, if you can guess my name, my real name, in three days, then you may have the child back."

She sank down on her bed. "Three days it is."

Three days later, Precious sat with her father. "But, Father, it's now the third day, and I've run out of names." Her shoulders slumped.

"Don't worry, my Precious. I have people everywhere trying to find it out."

There was a tapping at the door.

"Come in," commanded the duke.

A servant ran in, his breath ragged. "Sir, I have found out the name of the tall man. I observed him with the child, dancing around a fire. He said, 'Rooblefound is my name, and I am your forever father.'"

"Excellent," the duke said.

The queen clapped her hands. "Let him in."

The tall man walked in. The queen studied her nails and smiled. Then she listed the names that she had said the previous two days.

"But your majesty," the tall man said. "You've already said all those names. Do you not have anything new for me?" He looked out the window at the setting sun. "Your time is almost up." He turned to go.

"Wait," purred the queen. "One more try. Is your name...Rooblefound?"

The tall man stopped. He turned to the queen. He bowed. And then he smiled. "You fool, what makes you think I'd say my real name out loud around the likes of you and your kin?"

And with that, he disappeared. The tall man and the child were never seen again.

Fighting Dragons
by Robert Fyfe

    After fighting dragons, smashing giants and tackling ogres, this next challenge appeared to be just one step too far. What did people expect of her, for goodness sake? If Bella had known that this was to be her fate, she would have sat at home and done the house work for her overbearing stepmother.

    Bella sat glumly, staring absently at the forest and wished that she had thought carefully before setting out on this adventure. It had seemed so perfect when she had heard that the king had offered a chest of gold to the knight who rescued his son and heir, Prince Andrew. She had set off with a song on her lips and the Sun on her back.

    She had sneaked her father's armor from off its stand and taken Karain, his trusted stead, without fear of reprisal, for she had often borrowed them before to go on adventures. As she cantered through the forest towards the dark mountains, she remembered her adventures up until this day: the dragon she had fought to save her sister, leaping from the phoenix wearing nothing but a roar of triumph as they attacked from out of the bright of the Sun. She laughed as she thought of how she had pretended to have a great secret to tell the ogre, making him bend down and turn to hear her whisper, thus turning his gaze from her and the crystal dagger she had held behind her back. A tingle of excitement shivered through her as she remembered the unicorn as he had bowed to her allowing her to alight onto his back. His hair of light had sent small power charges through her fingers as she gripped with her hands and knees and they sped like lighting though the trees to save the fairy princess from the goblins.

This time she had found a fawn, who had seen the Prince being carted off by pixies, headed towards the caves on the shore of Lake Garma. When she arrived, she found that the caves were being protected by giant crabs, so she had sat on the dunes for almost three hours before she had a plan.

As the sun set and the tide turned inward to the shore, the wind picked up and the tops of the waves broke into white cap horses that stampeded into the caves, crushing the crabs and flooding the hollows they found. Upon the top, standing astride the back of two water spirits holding reigns of shipwrecked rope and wrapped only in folds of seaweed, stood Bella. With her sword held high, she shouted a challenge to the pixies who scattered in fear to the darkest recesses of the cave roof just long enough for Bella to grab the Prince who had been held in a magic trance ever since being kidnapped. The water spirits returned them to the shore, and Bella knew that to release the Prince all she had to do was kiss him.

Back at the castle, the King, hearing of her exploits and of Prince Andrew's love for the woman who had saved him, announced their engagement and sent for her father and stepmother.

At that moment Prince Andrew came into the room and looked at Bella. He was handsome and his smile warmed her cold heart.

'What's wrong Bella? I can see that something troubles you and I am saddened to see the shadow that covers your face.'

Bella looked at him and knew she could not lie. She told him that she liked him but that she did not want to marry him or anyone right now. She wanted the adventures and the excitement, and she didn't want the parties and fancy dresses or to be held in the Castle as a prisoner in a room that would feel like a cell, just for her safety or just to be there for his beck and call.

The Prince looked at Bella with warm eyes and then, after a moment, he burst into laughter. Not mocking or teasing, just joyful.

"Oh Bella, what fairy tales your father must tell of us royals. My father the king is just a big old romantic and means only good in this union. As for me, well I must be one too, as I fell in love with you the moment I saw you. As for holding you here against your will, then you have this all wrong."

"I promise you, Bella, we will not get married unless you desire it, and if we do, I promise that you will not be bound by the castle walls. You and I will seek adventure wherever it is to be found. I would never look to shackle such a life, for it is you I love, not some dream."

Bella looked into his face, jumped into his arms and whispered "I do."

Crimson
by Julia Lela Stilchen

    Father told me of the shifters that roam at night deep in the dark forests of Glenwood. When they gather in groups, their eyes ignite like blazing spheres lurking out from the shadows, searching for a new victim. Every day, before the sun would set, father closed all the windows of our cottage. He lit at least three candles in each room. Each specially made from dragon whale wax. The vapors burned red in a trail scented of wild wood. He said the smell would hide our scent so the shifters could not track us. One night, I blew out the candles and opened my window.

    I stared out into the blackness, waiting to see if I could spot a pair of shifter eyes. At one moment, I thought I heard a rustle of some kind. I leaned out from my window. The moon's light highlighted the edges of the leaves on the trees just beyond the yard. The cool breeze brushed against my skin, sending goose bumps up my arms. I heard a whisper of my name. I reached for my red shawl mother made for me. It was so long, it dangled at my feet. I wrapped it over my head to make a hood and cloak.

I crept quietly toward the hall leading downstairs. Father was snoring and mother was asleep holding the Good Book in her hands. I urged forward, making careful steps downward and avoiding the one wooden board that would bend and creak like old bones slowly breaking.

I slipped out the back door and turned my ear toward each soft hiss of my name, delicately tagging along the breath of the wind. I wasn't sure if I was still awake. Part of me felt scared and yet, a greater part of me was too curious. I wanted to know what was out there. Who was calling me? I was drawn under its spell, I could not resist.

I travelled what seemed like hours yet I hardly felt tired. The whispers faded and I no longer had a trail to follow. I rested near a pond and watched the moon reflected back in it. A small whimper rose from behind. I turned and saw a small wolf caught in a trap. His foot was injured and stuck. Lucky for him, it was too big to have caused serious damage, but caught him enough that he couldn't free himself. I pulled at the teeth on both sides, enough for the wolf to slip from its grip. He growled low to the ground, limping a few steps away from me. His eyes glowed like hot embers. Suddenly my head felt light and dizzy. All I remembered was falling to the coolness of soft grass.

The next morning, the villagers found me and brought me back home. Their faces were filled with fright, staring at me with panic. Their whispers echoed the words, "marked." Father and mother stood with mouths gaping. I watched as their expressions went from relief to gasping in horror. Mother fell to her knees and cried.

"I'm okay. I'm okay."

Father brought a mirror to my face. I looked closely. There were markings of some kind. Ancient glyphs and curving lines. What did it mean? Why was it there? I heard others whisper again. A curse they said, from the evil works of the night shifters. I was claimed. Claimed for what? Everyone agreed to banish me for the good of the village. Exiled.

I stood at the edge of the forest with a basket of food from mother, a silver cross from father and a map to Grandmother's house beyond Glenwood forest.

I was just a child. I did not feel any different from everyone else. Overnight, my life changed. I was no longer wanted in my home and forced to live with a grandmother I didn't know I had. I took my first step into the forest and into my new life, whatever it might hold for me.

Before
by Tia Mushka

Once there was a girl who looked up at the moon. The moment was magical and she wanted to keep it.

She sighed. "If only I could have a gown as white as the moon, I could remember the moon always."

This girl happened to be a princess, so the dress was made. It was as soft as whispering moonlight. She danced and whirled in the dress until it caught on a thorn, and it tore and she could wear it no more.

The girl was sad and folded the dress away.

She grew a little older. She looked down at the tulips blooming in the earth. She fell under their spell and wanted to stay. She sighed, "If only I could have a jewel as crimson as these flowers. Their petals will always be with me."

And because she was a princess, a jewel was found. It glittered on her neck as she played in her garden. She hid, and she ran, until one day it fell off, and bounced down a crack and was lost.

The girl's tears washed away in the wind.

The girl grew a little older and the princess had to travel to a far away land to marry a prince. She looked up at the sky and fell in love with the night. The moment was still and she wanted to hold it. She sighed, "If only I could have a horse as black as the night."

And because she was a princess, a horse was found. It was as dark as midnight, and just as wild. They tore through the towns and countryside until the horse broke free, and was gone.

A heart-broken hand waved goodbye.

The princess grew up, and she became the queen. The queen looked out at the world. It was winter and the snow fell like stars in the forest. The moment made her heart ache, and she pricked her finger on a sewing needle and spilt drops of blood in the snow. "Black branches, white snow, red blood. Oh, if only I could find something as black as the winter branches, as white as the snow, and as scarlet as blood. Something that would never tear, or fall, or run away. I would remember this beauty always."

And she did, and she loved her, and she named her Snow White.

Prince Peter

by Cecilia Clark

Prince Bruce swaggered in under the weight of his latest football trophy. King Archibald the Wealthy and Queen Beetroot the Beauteous, exclaimed loudly of his magnificence and physical prowess. Prince Bruce flexed his muscles and stuck out his chin to best show his profile for the ever present photographers.

Prince Eggbert, staggered in under the weight of his latest treatise and literary prize for genius. King Archibald and Queen Beetroot lauded his intellect and prattled praise to all the petitioners. The Royal framers were sent for immediately to preserve the wisdom. Eggbert flicked back a lock of his silken hair and lifted his golden glasses up his nose, ready for his interview with all the best journalists.

Prince Caruso plunged in under the weight of his latest bounty of bouquets and ribbons from his perfect performance of the prince in Swan Lake. Queen Beetroot swooned into the arms of proud King Archibald. The journalists and photographers turned from the first two princes to be first with an exclusive on the Royal dancing divo.

Prince Peter pondered his place in such a prestigious family. He couldn't play football, he wasn't super smart, he didn't dance and he doubted his parents even remembered his name. Prince Peter decided it was time to head out into the world and find his own special talent. He packed his bag and proceeded to say goodbye.

First he said goodbye to Lucy the Lady of the Bedchamber, asking her about her ailing father. He thanked her for all her delicate diligence and Lucy stifled a sob into a spotty handkerchief. Lucy later lamented that she would miss the youngest Prince and his kindness.

Then he said goodbye to the Lord Chamberlain. Prince Peter shook his hand and politely posited his opinion that the Chamberlain kept the Royal Household functioning better than any of his predecessors. The Lord Chamberlain cleared his throat to stop a particularly persistent catch and bowed respectfully to the Prince. The Chamberlain later confided to the Vice Chamberlain how considerate the young Prince was.

Prince Peter next thanked the Page of the Backstairs. He praised the Page's care of the personal apartments of the Royal Couple and promised he would send a postcard from his travels. The page pumped the Prince's hand in a hearty handshake. "Personally," the Page proclaimed in the servants' parlour, "I prefer Prince Peter over all his brothers."

The Astronomer Royal turned his gaze from the heavens to survey the Prince. "The stars are a road no one yet travels," he said. Prince Peter looked up at the stars in wonder, then nodded his head. "That boy always asked the very best questions," the Astronomer Royal said over his nightcap.

Prince Peter stopped to listen to the Master of Music and applauded appreciatively when the music ceased. The Master of Music bowed low in acknowledgement and sadly surprised at Prince Peter's news, promised to compose a piece in his honour to play if he ever returned. The Master of Music, in tones sombre and mellow, wished that Prince Peter just would not go.

Hissing and honking, the swans soon surrounded Prince Peter and Kevin the Keeper of the Swans. Kevin was troubled but put a brave face on in light of the news that the Prince would be gone.

Prince Peter patted the long skinny necks and plucked a bright feather to put in his hat. "I tell you," said Kevin, "this place will be sadder with our Prince Peter out in the world."

All of the servants, throughout the palace whispered the news that Prince Peter was leaving. Butlers and chambermaids, stable boys, cleaners, chimney sweeps, gardeners, tailors and chefs, keepers of roses and purses and secrets gathered with masons and woodsmen and hunters, all in the great hall to loudly protest. The King and the Queen and the other three princes sat up on their thrones to face the great throng.

"See here," said the king, "what is this nonsense?"

"What do you mean?" said the queen. "Peter's gone?"

"I need him here to hear all my strategies, to tell me the moves I best need to win. I will go find him!" Prince Bruce left, at a run.

"I need him here to hear my best arguments, to tell me if they are boring and long. I will go find him!" Prince Eggbert soon followed.

"I need him here. He is my best critic. I simply can't dance if my brother is gone. I will go find him!" Prince Caruso leapt out of his seat in a rush.

Prince Peter had stopped to consult with the stableboy; he knew him by name, to the stableboy's pride. Peter had saddled his favourite palfrey. Geoffrey the stallion was ready to ride.

Suddenly there was a rowdy commotion. The whole Royal Household was waiting outside. Peter led Geoffrey out of the stables and, at his appearance, there came a hush. The crowd started calling, including his brothers, all tumbling words of endearments and protest.

"You're still here," "thank goodness," "we need you," "we'd miss you," "please don't go," "you're very important," "the kindest," "the nicest," "the most thoughtful of princes," "handsome," "friendly," "simply the best," were all spoken to Prince Peter.

"Never assume," said the King, stern but loving, "that you are unimportant to us."

Prince Peter stood stunned. He never imagined that he would be missed. His brothers all hugged him. The servants all cheered. On his cheeks, by his mother, he was Royally Kissed.

Will the Stars Still Shine?
by Theresa Nielsen

Once upon a time in a little house at the bottom of the hill lived a young boy with his mom and dad and new baby sister.

It was just after dinner, and Timmy had finished his bath.

"Time for bed, Timmy. And don't forget to brush your teeth," said Mom.

Timmy stood on the stool in front of the sink. "Mom, will the stars ever stop shining?"

"Oh, I don't think so."

"Maybe if I pick up my toys, will they stop shining?' he asked.

Mom chuckled, "Probably not."

Mom tucked Timmy into his bed and gave him a kiss goodnight. "See you in the morning. I love you."

"I love you, Mom."

After the door closed, Timmy climbed out of bed. He took his blanket and pillow and curled up right under the window. He could see bright lights and tiny shining stars. Soon he drifted off to sleep.

After breakfast the next morning, Timmy helped Mom with the dishes.

"Mom, if the bluebirds fly all night and the owl hoots, will the stars stop shining?"

"I don't think so Timmy." Mom smiled and went off to feed the baby.

That night, the owl hooted and the birds flew from tree to tree. Yet the stars kept shining.

The next day, while walking home from the grocery store with Mom and the baby, Timmy asked, "Mom, if my baby sister cries and cries because she can't find her blanket, will the stars stop shining?"

"Even when babies cry at night, and they do, the stars will continue to shine."

"Well, well," said Timmy.

"Mom, if I shine my flashlight into the trees all night so the stars don't have to, do you think they will stop shining?" he asked.

"No Timmy, it's not very likely."

"Mom, can I stay up all night on my blanket out in the yard with you and Dad, and watch the stars shine all night?"

"You want to stay awake all night and watch the stars shine?" Mom asked.

"Yes," said Timmy. "And I want to see the moon glow and the sun come up."

"Okay," said mom. "We'll do it."

That night Timmy lay on his blanket next to Mom and Dad. His baby sister was asleep in her little seat on the blanket too.

"Look Mom," said Timmy, pointing up at the dark night sky. "I see the moon and the stars. They are so bright."

"Yes they are," said Mom. "Timmy, what is the name of that star high in the sky?"

But Timmy didn't answer, he was already fast asleep. And the stars continued to shine on and on all night long.

The next morning at breakfast, Timmy said, "Mom you're right. The stars will never stop shining. Can I go ride my bike now?"

"Yes Timmy, have fun."

That evening after dinner, Mom was folding laundry and the baby was sleeping on Dad's lap.

"Mom," said Timmy.

"Yes, what is it," she asked.

"Why do dogs bark?"

Mom only shook her head, but she didn't say a word.

Tom Thumb in Hot Water

by Yvonne Mes

Ever since Tom Thumb escaped from the belly of a cow and the paunch of a wolf he was a nervous wreck. His tiny body shook, his hands trembled and his thumbs twitched.

He had nightmares about horses, sheep, dogs, cats and chickens. Where, before, animals had been his best friends, now he feared anything bigger than a mouse.

"Poor Tom," his mother would sigh after another of Tom's bad dreams, as they started the day with milk and boiled eggs.

Tom never went outside; he was more at ease indoors with the cockroaches, who were just as much at home inside the house as they were out.

Slowly Tom relaxed, his body hardly ever shook, his hands stilled and he often gave a thumbs up without the tiniest twitch.

"Please, ask your new friends to move somewhere else," Mrs Thumb begged. "Our food is spoiling."

Tom was bored. He needed exercise and fresh air, but instead he hung out with the roaches and stole bacon from the larder.

This went on for many months, until one day Tom overheard the roaches discuss a most gruesome thing.

"Two teaspoons should be enough to make those Thumbs sleep forever," the roach leader said, swishing a foamy liquid in a glass vial.

Tom snuck closer.

"Slip it in their milk in the morning and the house will be ours, forever."

"No!" Tom screamed. He ran and reached for the vial. Too late and too slow!

Tom was captured and imprisoned in the worst place of all, the chicken coop. Tom's body shook so badly, his hands trembled so much, and his thumbs twitched so madly that he could not run and hide, but, instead, bopped up and down on the dirt without control.

The chickens gathered round.

"What is it?" said one.

"Can we eat it?" asked another.

"It must be a fat little worm," said a speckled hen.

"Then it will be all mine to devour," spoke the rooster.

Tom twitched and trembled even more furiously. He was about to be pecked and pickled when the speckled hen shouted, "Stop! That is Tom Thumb! Look, those are his little flailing hands and his little flailing feet. Worms don't have limbs!"

The rooster inspected Tom.

"We haven't seen Tom for years, not since the unfortunate incidence with the cow and the wolf." His beak swept down, grabbed Tom by the scruff and stood him up straight.

"We remember you, Tom Thumb, but do you remember us?" And Tom did. He remembered the games they used to play out in the sun, under the blue sky, and the crazy chicken dances they used to dance to the sound of the wind singing through the trees.

Tom stopped trembling, and, with a snap of his fingers, his last twitch disappeared, never to return.

This is when brave Tom Thumb came up with a gutsy plan. Holding a sharp rock, Tom was swallowed whole by the largest and fattest hen in the hen house, and overnight was enveloped in a shiny, fat egg.

Early in the morning his mother came to gather the eggs.

"This egg is just what we need to go with our breakfast," she said.

As soon as Tom heard his mother's voice he smashed the sharp rock he held against the inside of the egg. But the egg wouldn't break, no matter how hard he beat and scraped and banged.

"Mom! Dad! I am in here!" Tom shouted. But his voice was muffled by the thick shell. At any moment, he feared, he would be dropped into a pan of boiling water and served for breakfast. His grieving parents would drink the poisoned milk and the cockroach gang would rule the roost and the house. Tom gripped the rock in both hands and with an enormous BANG, hit the inside of the shell one last time.

Crickkkk-ety-crack.

A tiny crack appeared.

Tom felt a terrible shaking, but this time it was not his trembling body! It was Mrs Thumb smashing the egg against the side of a bowl, where Tom fell, splat, between the flour and milk, ready to be whipped into pancakes.

And that is how Tom escaped the belly of a chicken, warned his parents and saved the day.

And does Tom still shake?

He does. He quakes with laughter when he thinks about the roasted roaches the chickens had for breakfast that morning.

Jack and the Giant

by David Jamieson

A sickening thudding sound was the only sound echoing through Jack's ears as the ground shook under his feet while he was chased by an irate giant.

"Fe, Fi, Fo, Fum, I smell blood of a village man. Be he alive, be he dead, whichever it be, I'll be well fed. "

Jack ran straight under a root of a giant tree and started down the bean stalk, but the giant wasn't so lucky. His foot got trapped under the same root and he fell hard.

"You'll pay for that!" The giant ripped the tree from its root and threw it where he last saw Jack.

"That was close." As the tree flew past Jack, it soared towards the ground below. Jack was halfway down the Beanstalk when he was caught off balance. The giant made his descent, snapping branches underfoot with his immense size.

"Faster Jack, faster," he uttered to himself. He reached the bottom of the beanstalk and was shouting for his mother to bring his axe, but got no reply. He put the goose down and the sack it was in.

"Mother I need my axe!" Still, there was no reply. A glint caught his eye as he saw the axe embedded in a log that hadn't been cut just yet near the tree stump, where his axe usually sat.

"Mother!" Again, Jack got no reply. Jack started chopping at the main trunk while the giant was still making his way down. One after another, the tightly twisted vines making up the trunk started to break loose. The giant was half the way down when his weight did the rest. A loud SNAP alerted Jack to step back, letting the stalk and the giant head South towards Lake Moondarra, where with one almighty splash the giant fell, causing boats to become moored on land.

"Mother! Mother!! I did it! He's dead! We have all the gold we need now, Mother!!!"

Jack went behind the house. Maybe his mother was hanging out the daily washing. That was when he saw the tree the giant had thrown at him. His mother was lying unconscious for the tree had landed on her leg crushing it.

"Mother!" But it was no use. He ran to get his axe.

"Jack, Jack, is that you?" His mother spoke softly.

"Yes, Mother." Jack hit the trunk once with his axe, causing his mother to scream in pain.

"Jack, it's no use. Chop the leg off."

"Mom!"

"Please, just do it," she pleaded.

Jack mustered up incredible strength and with one single blow, Jack cut his mom's leg clean off.

"Use your belt to tie it off. Then go get Doc Farraday."

Jack raced off to get the doctor.

Jack was too late returning with Doc Farraday, and his mother died from blood loss. With his heart broken, Jack cried and cried. None of the riches he gained was worth his mother's life.

He gave all the riches away except enough to buy food and to buy weapons in case he ever came across another giant. Jack was once hungry for food, but now he missed his mother's love, and he was hungry for revenge.

Fairy Fractures
by Angelica Fyfe

In the twilight, time doth freeze.
The air goes still; there's nary a breeze.
Yet beyond the hill and beneath the trees
There lives a land of wonder.
At this time and at this place,
Things move by at an unusual pace.
A circle of mushrooms is the only trace
Of the world that flows just yonder.
Here is where the veil wears thin
Between reality and what lies within,
A step or stumble to enter in,
With the ground roaring like thunder.
Mischievous plants and folk so fae,
With mischievous grins and flutes to play,
All await in this place of surreal day,
Leaving all who visit to stop and ponder.
Many the poet, the artist, the bard
Hath tried to portray this little shard
Of a world where reality is not so hard
And the fae folk stay to plunder.
Alas, none can fully capture
A world such as this that can enrapture
All those on the other side of the fracture
To a world that we should not squander.

Lise & Nat
by Rebecca Fyfe

Lise was a child of the Sun. Its warmth and radiance favored her species of fairy, and she reveled in its light. One day, she was so engrossed in dancing and playing that the night fell upon her before she even realized it was getting late. Startled by the darkness creeping up and weakened from the lack of the Sun's rays, she turned for home but found her way blocked.

A tall figure stood before her. His skin was pale and his eyes were dark. He wore all black, shrouding himself in a cloak of shadows. He smiled at her and she stared at the fangs peeking out from his smile.

She knew about vampires. Just as her fae kind could enchant and ensnare humans, these blood-drinking dark counterparts could also capture human minds through enchantment. Lise tried to move past the vampire, but tripped on a stone and stumbled.

His strong arms caught her, keeping her from falling. She lifted her gaze to his. Instantly, they were both ensnared in each other's enchanted gazes. They kissed and sat speaking for hours. Lise learned that the vampire's name was Nat. Nat learned that Lise loved to dance. They soon fell in love.

Before long, the Sun began to rise and Lise realized that her beloved Nat was suffering. He could not live in her sun-filled world and she, a creature of the Sun, could not live in his eternal night. She cried out to her beloved Sun to help her but the Sun refused.

The spirit of the Forest heard her pleas and took pity on her. The Forest transformed Lise and Nat into oak trees, with their roots and branches forever entwined. They would be together forever as trees, nourished by the sunlight yet never harmed by the night.

Rapunzel
by Melissa Gijsbers

Glancing at the clock on the wall, Rapunzel calculated she still had time to work on her secret project before her mother arrived. She sneezed as dust flew up from where she was working.

"Not much longer," she muttered. She stretched her tired muscles as she prepared her bath. Her mother expected her to look like a princess should, even though she wasn't one, yet.

Brushing her hair and tying it in a long braid, she smiled to herself. The visit from the prince a few days earlier had made her more determined than ever to finish her project. Confident that the room was back to normal and her hair was ready, she picked up her book to wait for the familiar words.

"Rapunzel, Rapunzel, let down your hair." Rapunzel sighed, putting her book to one side.

"Coming Mother," she called down the tower before lowering her braid. She winced as her mother climbed her hair; she had put on weight recently. "Or she's brought me more goodies..." She knew it was wishful thinking.

"Phew," the old woman fell on the floor of her tower room. "That's a long climb." She wiped sweat from her forehead with a red handkerchief and dumped her backpack on the floor. "Supplies."

"Thank you Mother," Rapunzel answered through gritted teeth as she unpacked the staple goods she had brought. She wrinkled her nose at the rampion. Her mother never listened when she told her she couldn't stand rampion and she wanted to try something new. She smiled to her herself as she put flour and sugar in their containers. "Not much longer now."

The visit was mercifully short. Rapunzel had spent the time trying not to fidget or do anything that would give away her longing to leave this tower room, while at the same time trying to be polite to her mother until it was time for her mother to go.

"Rapunzel, Rapunzel, let down your hair." The familiar cry took Rapunzel by surprise. She had been so absorbed in her work she forgotten the time. She hurriedly tidied up and set about re-braiding her hair.

"Just a minute," she called as she finished her braids and threw them out the window. She winced again as the prince climbed up.

"My love," he greeted her as she pulled her braids back into the tower room. She stood quietly as he kissed her on the cheek. She was always disappointed there was none of the excitement she had read about in books. "Soon I shall find a way to get you out of here, and then we shall be married and will live happily ever after."

Rapunzel resisted the urge to roll her eyes.

"Of course we shall," Rapunzel was becoming the queen of telling people what they wanted to hear. This wasn't hard when she only ever saw two people – her mother and the prince.

Rapunzel sat quietly, listening to him tell her all about his latest exploits and everything that was going on in the palace. She didn't have much to tell him about her life for she spent all day in a single room at the top of the tower. Besides, the prince never asked.

It was sunset before the prince left, and it was getting too dark to do much more on her secret project. She settled down to her simple dinner, itching to get back to work. She would have to wait until the next morning. At least there would only be one visitor tomorrow. She was so close.

That night, Rapunzel fingered the scissors that were hidden under her pillow. They were an accidental item her mother had left in the bottom of her bag during one of her visits.

"Funny," Rapunzel thought. "If it hadn't been for these, I never would have thought to start my project."

A few days later, Rapunzel heard the familiar cry, "Rapunzel, Rapunzel, let down your hair." She giggled and ran her fingers through her newly styled bob, threw her braid out the window and anchored it securely. Skipping down the brand new staircase, she headed toward the hole she had made at the base of the tower.

As she ran through the woods, she could only imagine the look on the prince's face as he got to the top of the tower to find her gone.

Midnight's Tale
by Brenda A. Harris

In the central woods of England, lived a family with two daughters. One was beautiful and harsh like the desert sun, while the other was as blue and lonely as a starless night. Their names were Sunshine and Midnight. Sunshine was fair of skin like her parents but not Midnight. She was unlike her family, because she had been found in the forest.

The mother loved both girls equally, but the father thought Midnight monstrous. He despised her and enjoyed ridiculing her. "Midnight, can't you do something with that porcupine mange of yours? If only you looked more like Sunshine, rather than the blue beast that you are, it might be easier to marry you off."

Upon hearing his cruel words, Midnight ran off into the woods to find solace. The woods comforted the girl; it was there she felt free to sing out her sorrows.

Today however, the woods warned her of fast approaching horses. Midnight hid and watched as a gallant knight and his squire galloped by. Not long after, she heard a loud thud and the sound of halting horses. Silently, Midnight made her way to where they were. She found the knight lying lifeless on the ground and his squire kneeling beside him in despair.

"Sir Galfridus, please awake," said the squire, but the knight gave no reply.

"Forgive me," said Midnight. "I don't mean to pry, but if I may be of service…"

Frightened by Midnight's appearance, the squire grew faint. However, her gentle demeanor soon gave him hope. Addressing her, he said, "A branch has struck my knight leaving him near death. He is in such grave a manner, I dare not travel with him, nor dare I leave him here for he will surely die. Alas, our misfortune," he continued, "for we carry an urgent message to our king."

Midnight offered to care for the knight, and the squire agreed. He carried his master to her cottage before leaving on his errand. As promised, Midnight attended to the knight. Father however, saw his chance to marry off Sunshine.

The next day, the knight awoke to blindness. Although he remained blind, his health recovered quickly with the help of Midnight's gentle hands. His heart began to warm to Midnight, and for the first time, Midnight felt the love of a man.

"Don't start thinking Sir Galfridus will marry you, Midnight. His sight will come back, and he will despise you all the more because of the love he has felt for you," said Father.

Sunshine laughed. "Wait and see, Midnight. When Sir Galfridus looks upon you, he will fall right into my arms."

Just as foretold, the knight's sight returned. When Midnight approached, he gasped. "Where is my beautiful maiden, the one who has cared for me and won my heart?"

"I am here," said Midnight.

"No, it can't be," he cried with broken heart.

"My dear knight," lied Sunshine, "I have sat here by your bedside waiting for you to recover."

The knight looked upon Sunshine's beauty. "Oh, my heavenly dove, you are as gorgeous as a sunny day. He professed his love for her and asked Father to bless their union in marriage. Aghast, Midnight fled, determined to live her life in her beautiful woods. Amidst the forest trees, she sang her sad song until all sorrow left her.

Later, in the middle of the night, a shadowy figure introduced himself to her. "I am Midnight," he said. "I listened to your woeful song, not daring to disturb you until now. May I ask how a beautiful damsel can be so sad?"

Startled, Midnight rose. "My name is Midnight, also. I am called that, because my skin is so dark blue."

The young man spoke with hope in his voice. "When I was a child, a wicked warlock stole our baby princess. She was called Nightingale. We have never found her."

Midnight took a better look at the man before her. "Your skin is as blue as this night," she said, "and your hair is as straight as the quills of the porcupine. You are like me!"

Hand in hand, the young man led her to his people. There, Midnight was bestowed her true name, Princess Nightingale. Her parents, the king and queen, rejoiced to have their daughter back. She reigned with them in wisdom and humility and was loved by all.

Toadly Awesome
by C. S. Frye

Rupert sat near a huge fountain in the courtyard. He watched as people walked hand in hand. *Why am I the loneliest frog in the world?*

Kittens played tag on the grass. *I wish I had someone to play with.*

Birds swooped and dooly-hooped. *Drats. Being a frog stinks!*

Rupert sang. "Ribbet! Ribbet! Ribbet! But no one answered. No one wanted to talk to a sad frog.

Someday, I'll have lots of friends.

Year after year, Rupert sang alone. One day a girl appeared at the fountain. She came back every day. She was the most beautiful girl Rupert had ever seen, but she was always sad. She cried from the minute she came until she left.

Rupert's hopes soared. *Oh, I wish I weren't a frog all green and fat. I would rather be a Prince with a feather in my hat.*

Soon the water was salty from the girl's tears. Rupert's eyes burned. He jumped from the pond into her pocket. He didn't croak. He didn't ribbet. *I hope for my wish to come true, that I'll become human, and she'll see me anew.*

The Princess hurried to the castle and up to her room, Rupert held his breath. She fell on her bed and cried quietly. Soon she fell asleep, and Rupert peered out of the pocket. *Where am I? I must run from here before I die!*

Stone walls hid the trees. The weird ceiling had no sky. There was no grass or stars, no kittens or birds.

Rupert eased out of her pocket. He crawled near her. When she whimpered, he stopped. He crept upon her pillow and squatted. Wispy strands of golden hair framed her face. A tear dropped from her wet lashes. The tear left a trail down her cheek to her lips. Rupert heaved a sigh. *How could someone so sweet be so sad? I wish I were a comely lad.*

He leaned forward. *If only I were human, I could dry those tears. I would guard her life and vanquish her fears.*

She smelled like lily pads. Rupert inched closer. He touched her lips to wipe away the tear -- but his touch morphed into a kiss. The Princess's eyes flashed open.

Rupert leaped from the pillow. The princess didn't scream, instead, her eyes gleamed with joy. She smiled. For the first time in his life, Rupert was speechless.

A veil of gray shrouded the room. Rupert squeezed his eyes shut. *Oh no! This is too scary! I want to go back home, and I cannot tarry!*

When he opened his eyes, the Princess was gone.

Croak!

But, on the pillow sat the most beautiful frog in the land.

At last, a frog his size. His dream had come true, there wasn't one frog, now there were two.

They joined arms and hopped out of the castle. They hopped until they reached the pond. Rupert jumped for joy. *I love my pond, I love my tree, no other frog is as happy as me!*

Now Rupert sings a happy song, but he never sings alone.

Dicky and the Dragon
by Elizabeth Gallagher

There is a legend – or more of a rumor actually, that dragons were once humans. Very, very cranky humans.

Dickey Diamond, a curious boy of 10, loved his parents very much and they loved him right back. Dan, Dickey's dad, was a hard worker at the Pufftone Marshmallow factory. Inez, Dickey's mom, was a nail technician down at Betty's Bob-N-Wave who was known for her long painted nails and fabulous hairdos.

It all started one fine sunny day when Dan accidentally slept in and was late to work. The marshmallow factory manager, though usually a nice man, had been bitten by his pet parrot that morning. The angry manager threw a handful of marshmallows at Dan, which immediately stuck to his shiny red hair. Dan was embarrassed that he was late AND had marshmallows stuck in his hair, so he just got crankier as the day wore on.

Later that afternoon when his mom and dad sat silently reading the paper, Dicky noticed a sparkling rainbow colored feather sprouting out of his dad's hair. *Curious*, thought Dickey.

Dan got crankier and found at least one thing to be mad about each day. One morning he got his face stuck in the hairspray that secured Inez's tall hairdo into its swirly shape while kissing her as he was leaving for work. Hot water separated Dan's face from Inez's hair, but he bellowed anyway as he left for work. When Dan let

Dickey out of the car at school that same morning, he kissed his son on the forehead and Dickey noticed that pearly scales covered half of his dad's face. Next it was Dickey's scooter left in the driveway that popped two of the new whitewall tires on his dad's car, and that night at dinner each time his dad breathed a tiny cloud of sooty smoke puffed out of Dan's mouth. *Interesting*, thought Dickey.

Dickey was relieved when Inez finally noticed that something was different about Dan. When they went to parties, it was Dan's now plentiful pearly scales and soft colored feathers that overshadowed Inez and her presently pink hairdo. She would huff and puff at Dan and drum her long lavender fingernails on whatever was nearby. Dan huffed and puffed right back even crankier than before, but his huffs and puffs began to carry little sparks of flame in them. Soon Dan was setting small fires around the house. He set the lawn on fire, and six fire trucks came. Dan got even crankier.

When Dan woke up in the morning about a month later, he was startled by the cat who was surprised by Dan's new look, and fell out of bed striking his head on the lamp. He banged the floor hard with his hand and stomped into the bathroom. After a calming shower, Dickey's dad tried to put on a shirt and tie. Neither stretched around his thick neck, and each time he tried to button the front, his long claws tore the buttons right off. Dan went to work that day without a shirt, but no one noticed because his chest was covered in shiny rainbow colored scales and down his back ran a line of large points.

Dan had a hard time fitting his body into his little car with the white wall tires, but fitting himself into his tiny office at work was truly a challenge. He had to bend way down to avoid hitting his head on the top of the doorway, and he had to kind of jiggle his big round belly from side to side to sit in his chair. When Dan sat down, he heard an awful wheezing and whining sound and looked down just in time to see the chair crack and fall apart under him. Lying there on the floor of his office without a shirt, with rainbow colored feathers sticking out of his hair, with large points rising out of his back and steam puffing out of his nose, Dan got even crankier. Suddenly, without any warning at all, a tail popped out of the seat of Dan's pants. In the blink of an eye, out of his shoulders popped two pearly wings. He left immediately with his friends laughing and pointing. That time they noticed!

Dickey was sitting in the front yard playing with a ball when his dad flew into the driveway. Dan just sat in the driveway with his large head in his clawed hands. Dickey ran over and jumped onto his dad's belly. "What's wrong, Daddy?" he asked in a tiny voice.

"Oh Dickey" said Dan Diamond, "I've really done it now."

Dickey looked into his dad's eyes and kissed him on his scaly cheek. "It's ok, Dad" Dickey said, "I love you! You're my Dad!" Dan and Dickey sat for awhile just being together, and then they tossed the ball around until Inez got home from the Bob-N-Wave.

At Dickey's Boy Scout Camporee that very weekend, Dan started all the campfires with his fiery breath, gave rides to all the kids that didn't get airsick, and led them on a couple of night hikes with his pearly skin glowing like a lantern. Dan was very popular at barbecues, and Inez basked in all the attention. For a while, his friends asked Dickey what he'd do if his dad stayed a dragon, but Dickey didn't wonder anymore. He knew. "Doesn't matter either way", he'd say, "I love him. He's my Dad!"

Spring Folly

by Jackie Castle

    Spring arrives, dropping her bags at the door with a loud bang. She shakes the dew from her clothes, splattering the earth with scattered drops. One look around at Autumn's artistic forays along with Winter's wild party blast and Spring knows she has her work cut out.

    Every year, she returns to the same mess: Autumn is such a show off, painting the leaves into brilliant colors before casting them off like crumpled sheets of paper. Winter, of course, is too busy bullying everyone with his cold blast to be of any help. Instead of taking a moment to sweep away some of Autumn's cast-offs, he throws a blanket of snow down to cover it up.

    Then there's Summer, Miss Lazy-Dog-Days herself. Summer isn't really a mess maker, unlike those other two. However, she is a bit persnickety about keeping things in quiet order. Which is why Autumn and Spring have to maintain some space between Summer and Winter. If they don't moderate the situation, Winter's rowdiness will send Summer into all manner of stormy hysterics.

    Summer, for the most part, enjoys sitting around like an old mother hen, heating up the earth. Oh, every once in a while, her feathers get ruffled for some reason or another, and she'll stir up an impressive thunderstorm. This generally happens when Winter gets restless and blows a cool front her way to disrupt her peaceful season. He can be such a scamp.

No, Summer prefers to sit and roost, drinking iced tea and relaxing beneath the sun as she watches the grass turn brown.

So, that leaves the cleaning to Spring. Ah well, she is quite used to it by now. She comes prepared to roll up her sleeves and get to work. First, she'll whip up the winds, blowing the debris left over from Winter's parties with the Chill brothers, Frost and Snow.

Yes, out it goes, old leaves, trash, hats, umbrellas—all blown into hither and beyond. After sweeping, she brings the buckets and mops from storage and washes and scrubs. Finally, she walks outside one morning and realizes how wonderfully everything shines.

Spring will then pause, catching her breath as she admires her handiwork. Oh, what's this?

Winter has had one more soirée in the Northern regions. Grumbling, Spring starts all over again— blowing, scrubbing, rinsing, and chastising Winter for infringing on her season. What nerve! She'd be sure to send him a calendar for Christmas with everyone's seasons circled. Oh wait, she did that last year. And the year before.

Spring sighs, knowing such is Winter's ill-mannered ways. Another reason Spring tries hard to make sure everything is in place before Summer arrives. If she didn't, the hot/cold war would rage and the poor people would be left wearing coats and shorts all in the same day. Such chaos!

Eventually, Winter traipses off to bed, needing to sleep away the effects of his merry-making. Spring checks her clock and hurries to add her own special touches. Autumn isn't the only talented one in the family. Spring sings a happy tune, as she sets out her blooming decorations. The earth is soon covered in deep greens, magenta, yellows, purples, and blues.

Once everything is cleaned up and in place, Spring collapses in exhaustion, surveying all her work. She no more than sets out a tray of tea and biscuits before the door flies open. Summer bustles in, fanning her sweating face as she drops her bags in the foyer.

"Well, here's a fine how-do-you-do. Is this how you spend your days? Sitting back with a pretty cup of tea and dainty biscuits while you kick up your heels and relax? Tut, tut. I came in the nick time. Things need heating up around here."

And so it goes…

The Sacred Scepter
by Nicole Zoltack

Emma hated going to her grandma's. Grandma pinched her cheeks too hard and hugged her tight so she couldn't breathe. She smelled funny too. Emma never knew what to say to her either.

And now she was stuck here for an entire week.

"Do you want something to eat?" Grandma asked.

"I'm not hungry. I'll just play in the backyard."

So many plants and flowers. She skipped on the stone path, then twirled in a circle with her arms outstretched, her eyes closed.

Something soft touched her arm.

Emma kept still as she opened her eyes.

It wasn't a butterfly.

It was a small creature. With sparkling wings. And a small crown on her tiny head. Purple hair. Orange eyes.

"Who are you?" Emma asked.

"Who are you?" the creature asked.

"I'm Emma."

"Nice to meet you, Emma. I'm Amie. A fairy."

"A fairy? Can you fly?"

"Of course!" Amie flew and twirled and danced around Emma. The two laughed. The fairy hovered inches from Emma's face. "Emma, human girl, I need your help. Our sacred scepter is missing."

Emma glanced around the garden. She had no idea what a scepter was.

She turned back to the fairy, but Amie was gone.

"Emma, I made cookies!" her grandma called.

Emma loved cookies but she only ate one as she joined her grandma in the house. "Grandma, what's a scepter?" she asked, shaking her head when Grandma held out the silver tray.

"Why do you ask?"

Her grandma wouldn't believe her. "I heard it…somewhere."

"A scepter is a staff."

Now that Emma knew what to look for, she raced back outside. She searched under the bushes and found a rabbit.

She searched in the flowers and discovered a butterfly.

She searched in the grass, and a beetle jumped and landed on her nose.

She struggled to climb up a tree. A bird flew around her, and she managed to climb to the top. Only leaves and a bird's nest were up here.

Ready to cry, Emma climbed back down. Amie had asked her for help. She had failed.

"What's wrong?" her grandma asked.

Emma was too upset to hold back any longer. "I can't find Amie's scepter."

"Do you want me to help look for it?"

She nodded. While her grandma looked in all the places she had already, Emma went inside her grandma's cottage. She found spoons with holes in them and brushes and rulers, but no scepters.

She accidentally knocked over a spice container and cleaned it up, using the last of the paper towels. The paper towel roll gave her an idea.

Emma colored a piece of paper and sprinkled it with glitter. Next, she attached it to the paper towel roll and added colorful ribbons to the top. Then she went back outside.

Her grandma was looking in a bush. "I'm sorry, I didn't find—now that's a scepter!"

Emma smiled. "Thanks!"

But it wasn't the fairies' lost one.

Her smile turned upside down.

"I'll go get the cookies. I'm sure you and Amie will like some." Grandma disappeared into the cottage.

Emma closed her eyes and twirled again as she had before Amie appeared the first time. And as before, Amie came.

"Did you find it?"

She swallowed and shook her head, then held up her makeshift scepter.

Amie flew up to it, and around it, and through the hole in the middle. "It's not our missing scepter, but it will work. That is, if you will give it to us."

"Of course!"

Amie clapped her hands, then flew over Emma's head. Fairy dust landed on her hair and face. Emma laughed and laughed and floated into the air for a few minutes.

When her feet touched the ground again, Amie and the scepter were gone.

"Here are the cookies." Grandma glanced around. "Where's your friend?"

Emma helped herself to one. "She's a fairy."

Grandma winked. "I knew you would eventually see them."

Emma's eyes widened. Grandma pinched her cheek, but it wasn't too hard. Emma was the one to hug her a little too tight. And Grandma smelled like cookies.

Maybe Emma had made more than one friend this day.

The Three Little Cherry Trees
by Linda Schueler

Once there were three little cherry trees. Above them on a hill lived an older cherry tree. They used to watch this cherry tree and sigh over her beautiful blossoms. "We can't wait until we have our own flowers," they said.

The year that they first started to produce blossoms, the little cherry trees cheered and laughed. "My, how beautiful you look, Darling," they would say to each other and giggle. The older cherry tree would look down upon them and smile.

But there happened to be a fox that lived nearby, and this fox was not smiling. "I am old now," he said to himself. "I just want quiet. No noisy bees, birds or cherry pickers." He stood and stared at the cherry trees. Then a grin spread across his face, from ear to ear.

The next day the fox approached the first little cherry tree. "My dear, if you want to keep that beauty, then you will have to close your blossoms to those bees and butterflies."

The old cherry tree rustled her leaves at the fox. "Go away, Fox. That is not our way."

The fox wrapped its tail around the little tree. "Don't listen to her. See how messy her blossoms are. She lets every creature make her look ugly. But you don't have to be like her."

And the first little cherry tree looked at the old one. "You are right, my fox friend." And so she closed her blossoms and shook her branches anytime an animal tried to land on them.

The old cherry tree's branches drooped. But the first little cherry tree said to her cherry tree friends, "Look how beautiful my blossoms are. You should do the same as I do." But the other two cherry trees just frowned at her.

So a while later the fox came back and wrapped his tail around the second little cherry tree. "I have a wonderful potion that I can rub on your bark that will keep you young forever. Not only will your blossoms stay young and fresh, but your bark will stay smooth."

Again the old cherry tree rustled her leaves at the fox. "That is not nature's way, Fox. Be gone."

"Are you going to listen to that old crone over there, with her cracked bark? You don't want to look like her, do you?" the fox purred.

And the second little cherry tree looked long and hard at the old tree. "You are right, my fox friend. Go ahead and rub on your potion."

The old cherry tree's branches drooped farther. And the two little cherry trees jeered at their third friend, "Look how young and beautiful we are. Come and join us." But the third little cherry tree frowned at them.

And the old cherry tree and the third little cherry tree dropped their blossoms. Soon little green orbs dotted their branches. Still the others mocked the third little cherry tree. "You could have stayed like us forever," they jeered.

The fox then approached the third cherry tree. "Do you want to have the biggest, most beautiful cherries? Give me your green ones and I will make them to be the best."

Again the old cherry tree rustled her branches. "Don't listen to this fox. What he says is not our way."

The fox wrapped his tail around the third little cherry tree. "Do you want to be like her, with tiny fruit? Or do you want me to help you to make the biggest fruit ever?"

And the third little cherry tree looked a long time at the old tree. And then she dropped her fruit.

And the fox took the fruit and said, "It will take some time, but I will return with your fruit after I am done."

And the old cherry tree's branches sagged a little further.

One day the cherry pickers came. And they looked at the two little cherry trees with blossoms. "There is something unnatural about them." And they took out their axes and chopped them down.

"Quick Fox, give me back my cherries," yelled the third little cherry tree. But there was no reply.

The pickers looked at the third tree, "This one is not useful to us." And they chopped her down too.

The old cherry tree's branches drooped so much, they almost touched the ground. But the fox, well the fox, he slept on in his den.

A Name and a Wish

by Ashley Howland

"Is your name Conrad?"
The horrid little man shook his head.
"Is your name Harry?"
"No" he shrieked with delight.
"Is your name Nigel?"
At the sound of the last name, Rumplestiltskin grabbed the baby girl and darted out the window.

The kingdom was thrown into despair and poverty. Meanwhile the girl became a slave to Rumplestiltskin. Her days were spent cleaning, preparing meals and listening to Rumplestiltskin sing. He was forever boasting about his name and how clever he was. By night she had to polish the treasure. Each night before she set to work her master would lock his most precious items in a cupboard. As the girl got older her curiosity grew about her past and the way she was drawn to the magical castle on the distant hill.

One night when she was polishing the gold she heard an argument outside. Rumplestiltskin was doing his usual trick. He had asked them to guess his name. Of course they got it wrong. After much arguing the man handed over his special item. A lamp.

"It could be worse," said Rumplestiltskin, "I once tricked the queen into handing over her first born daughter."

He chuckled as he walked into the house. The girl quickly moved away from the window and continued to polish the treasure. She had always thought she belonged somewhere else. Now she knew her rightful home was the castle.

Rumplestiltskin entered the room, singing and laughing to himself. He placed the lamp in the cupboard and turned to leave.

"You're very happy," said the girl as she moved closer to Rumplestiltskin, removing some straw from his hair.

"Of course, I have won again," said Rumplestiltskin, as he danced out of the room.

He never noticed that the girl had stolen the key from his jacket.

Quickly the girl opened the cupboard and took out the mysterious lamp. It was covered in dirt, so she rubbed it with her rag.

To her surprise a puff of sparkly steam flew out the spout, magically turning itself into a humongous smoking genie. The Genie filled the room and began to speak.

"You have three wishes."

The girl came up with a plan.

"My first wish is the skill to spin straw into gold," she said.

"Granted," said the genie.

The girl ran over to the spinning wheel and tried out her new skill. She spun straw into the most perfect golden chain.

"My second wish is to become the most beautiful butterfly, so beautiful that people will always follow me."

With a flick of his wrist the girl became a butterfly.

"Now my third wish is to be transported back in time," said the girl. She then quickly whispered the last part of her plan.

The Genie smiled and her world began to spin.

The sun shone brightly. Rumplestiltskin was dancing and singing a merry tune in front of his house. He never noticed a beautiful butterfly leaving his treasure room.

The butterfly flew to the castle. There in the grounds was the Queen, with her precious baby girl. Through her tears she read out a list of names. None of them were right. Then suddenly she looked up and saw the most beautiful butterfly. The Queen stood and walked closer, the butterfly flew off down the hill. The Queen followed.

There in front of a strange little house was the horrid little man, singing to himself. The Queen listened and smiled. Now she knew. The butterfly followed her back to the castle.

"I have come to collect my prize," laughed Rumplestiltskin.

"I have three guesses left," said the Queen.

Rumplestiltskin rolled his arm gesturing for her to continue.

"It is Conrad?" she asked.

He shook his head.

"Is it Harry?"

"No!" he shrieked with delight.

Is it....Rumplestiltskin?" asked the Queen with a smile.

He suddenly disappeared in a flash, never to be seen again. Instantly, the butterfly became a beautiful jewelled charm.

The Queen picked up the charm and placed it on her beautiful baby as she named her Butterfly.

As Butterfly grew, she spun straw into gold, ensuring the Kingdom remained prosperous. They all lived happily ever after.

Cindy and Ella
by Cecilia Clark

Cindy had a good life. She had big sisters, Stacy, 15 and Lu, 16. Even if they were stepsisters they let her borrow makeup and pretty shoes and said she could use their wardrobe full of dresses.

Her step mother, Angie, was nice. Dad was away a lot with work but when he came home he tried to make up for it by taking them all to the movies and theme parks. He bought so many presents, it was better than birthdays. Angie became sparkly when Cindy's Dad came home. It was all romance and kisses with them. Cindy found it all a little icky.

Then Angie announced she was having a baby. Dad was thrilled. The step sisters were disgusted as only big sisters can be, and Cindy was worried. Dad reorganised his work so he could be home more often. Stacy and Lu spent more and more time staying over with their friends. Dad took Cindy aside and asked her to help Angie all she could when he was away. Cindy was left to do all the chores which Stacy and Lu were not home for and Angie was too sick to do.

"Cindy can you make me a cup of tea?"
"Cindy can you hang out the washing?"
"Cindy can you get me a bucket?"

Cindy ran to fetch a bucket and then a glass of water and then a cool face cloth. As Angie got bigger and bigger, Cindy got to do more chores. When Dad was home, he sorted the bills, bought the groceries, mowed the lawn and went to the clinic with Angie. The presents and movies stopped and the baby things came instead.

Stacy and Lu came home for clothes, their text books and usually left again with a yell of 'Home work at Teah's' or 'study at the library' and a final, 'we'll eat out.'

Cindy started making the evening meal for her and Angie. She would look up recipes on the internet to find things pregnant women could eat and then check the cupboard for the ingredients. If there was something she needed she would put it on the shopping list for Dad to buy.

Then she learned how to use the washing machine because Angie was just too big to reach into it. Cindy tried to do her own homework too but she had a lot of housework to keep up with.

All the time, she worried. This baby was going to be Dad and Angie's and the stepsisters were Angie's and Dad was Angie's now too. So she, Cindy didn't belong to anyone anymore and she didn't know if they would even want her when the baby arrived. She took the washing off the line and folded it neatly, then went to her room to do some homework.

"Cindy, can you run me a bath?" Cindy sighed and closed her math book. She turned on the water and poured in Angie's favourite salts, she hung the towels on the rail and lit a scented candle. Angie waddled in, her robe barely covering her swollen abdomen. Cindy wasn't sure how long it took for babies to grow but it looked like Angie was ready to burst. Cindy stayed to help her into the bath.

Suddenly Angie was calling for Cindy to fetch the phone. "Call your Dad quick."

Everything happened in a rush then. The ambulance came. Stacy and Lu ran in and left for the hospital straight after. Cindy was left at home alone. Dad said he would come and fetch her and she waited and worried.

Finally a car arrived and Dad ran in. "It's a girl Cindy, another beautiful girl." He swung her up in the air like he used to do when she was little and hugged her tight. "Come meet your baby sister."

Cindy gazed at the tiny wrinkled baby in the hospital crib.

"Her name is Ella." Angie smiled and held her arms open to hug Cindy." You will be the best big sister. Thank you for all your help. I am so happy I am part of your family."

A wave of magic flowed through Cindy and her worries melted away. "My family."

The best kind of magic is Love.

The Raven Girl
by Rebecca Fyfe

Rhianna kept her eyes on the sleek, black raven as it perched on the rail of her porch. The stories the old ones told about ravens was that finding one alighting on your home was an omen of either a death in the house or a great change to come. She tried shooing the beast away, but it wouldn't budge; it just sat there, calmly gazing back at her. Giving up, she turned away and moved further into her house to check on her brother.

Just two years older than her, her brother Connor had always been the strong one, looking out for her. But now, he was the one who needed her. The soldiers had come and when they tried to take her, he had fought. When he was bloody and broken on the ground, they had left her alone. He wasn't expected to live.

She checked on his sleeping form in the bed, could see the droplets of sweat breaking out on his reddened, feverish skin. He wasn't getting any better. An image of the raven on her porch invaded her mind but she quickly dismissed it. Her brother was going to get better; she wouldn't allow him not to.

She made him some tea and, as she walked from the kitchen to bring it to him, her attention was drawn to the porch again. The porch now held three ravens. The shock of it almost had her dropping the mug of tea. She moved to the door and pushed the screen open.

"You can't have him! There'll be no death in this house!" She raged at the black creatures. The ravens rustled their feathers but didn't budge from their perches. Rhianna sighed and felt a bit silly. Why had she thought yelling at the birds would help?

As night fell, Rhianna felt a chill fall over the house. She knew she couldn't leave her brother's side, not this night. She pulled a chair over beside his bed, facing the window and she sat to watch over him. He moaned a little in his sleep, making her feel helpless, unable to ease his suffering.

A dark smoke began to fill the room and as it thickened, it began to form a shape. Within moments, a woman wearing a gown of black feathers and a crown made of bones stood before her.

Rhianna looked her over. Her hair was black and her eyes were dark, but her skin was quite pale. It was the Morrigan.

"I hear you have been defiant today," the woman purred. "But you must know that it is his time. I'm here to take him on the next part of his journey."

"So it is to be death then, not change," Rhianna said. "I won't allow it. I will fight you for him."

"Fight me? I have millennia of experience in battle. Are you so sure you can win?" The woman's voice sounded grating to Rhianna's ears, like the cawing of crows. But there was a calculating look in her gaze. Rhianna knew she shouldn't trust her. But what choice did she have?

"No, but I cannot let him go. He's my brother, and I love him." Rhianna's voice trembled despite the bravado of her words.

"Then so be it. If you win, your brother will be allowed to live, but you must take my place, collecting souls when it is their time and delivering them to the afterlife. But if you lose, I shall take both yours and your brother's souls tonight."

"So be it." Rhianna agreed.

"Then you win," the elegant lady said, smirking in triumph before Rhianna had even stood up, disappearing in a swirl of smoke.

And Rhianna felt herself change. She watched as her clothes changed to the blackest of black and a crown of bones formed on her head. Her long blonde hair darkened to midnight black, and as she watched, the skin on her hands grew paler. She was now the Morrigan, a warrioress, forever in service to the dead.

But that wasn't the end of the changes. Along with her new life collecting souls and influencing battles, her brother would forever be by her side. He was still alive, as the Morrigan had promised, but he had transformed into a raven. And he would remain, trapped in raven form, serving by her side, forever.

The Princess and the Pea
by Melissa Gijsbers

Theresa tossed and turned in her bed. This was one of the strangest beds she had ever slept in; she had to climb a ladder to get to the top. She fluffed her pillow, hoping that it would help.

"I only wanted somewhere dry to sleep," she muttered. "And now I'm sleeping on the top of Mount Mattress."

She just couldn't get comfortable. Sitting up, she realised that there was something under the mattress. Theresa reached over and felt under the first mattress, nothing there.

"One down, Forty to go." She carefully climbed onto the ladder and felt under each mattress. "There has to be something under there," she muttered as she reached under number nineteen. By the time she was two thirds down, the mattresses were threatening to fall on the floor.

At three quarters of the way down, Theresa yawned, wanting to sleep, but convinced there was something keeping her awake. Determined to work out what it was, she kept going.

"This is the strangest place I've been," she said to herself, remembering the reception when she arrived at the door of the castle dripping wet from the storm was interesting to say the least. She had reluctantly admitted to being a real princess, one of the strangest questions she had ever been asked. Almost immediately she had been whisked away to a room to dry out, given a meal and then brought to this strange bedroom.

"Ah, hah!" she cried triumphantly as she discovered three small peas under the bottom mattress. She pulled them out, climbed carefully back up the ladder and curled up under the quilts, plumping her pillow, and falling into a deep sleep, the peas clasped in her hand.

The next morning, Theresa was woken by knocking on the door and a maid coming in with a cup of tea.

"The king, queen and prince are expecting you in the throne room for breakfast as soon as you are ready." The maid curtsied, waiting to one side for Theresa to climb down the ladder. A gown was hanging on a hook on the wall, inviting Theresa to wear it. She sipped her tea and started to get ready for her audience with the royal family with the assistance of the maid.

"My dear, how did you sleep?" the queen asked as Theresa sat down at the long banquet table. The prince winked at her and the king ignored her.

"It took a while, but eventually, I had a wonderful sleep," Theresa replied honestly. She savored the smells of the food in front of her before taking a bite.

"Really?" The prince tried to keep the disappointment out of his voice.

"The bed I was in is the weirdest bed I've ever slept in," she took another bite of her breakfast.

"Are you sure you had a good sleep?" the queen asked.

"I'm sure,"

"That's that, then," the queen announced, wiping her mouth and standing up from the table, "The hunt continues." Theresa sat quietly, finishing her breakfast before asking for her own clothes to be returned so she could be on her way.

As she was leaving the castle, she said, "I believe these are yours." She dropped three peas into the queen's outstretched hand before turning to continue on her journey. She missed the look of surprise on the queen's face as she skipped down the path to continue her adventure.

How Shadow Saved His Fairy
by Brenda A. Harris

Long ago, there lived a warlock named Thames and his wicked wife Tasha. They abhorred housework. So, after years of arguing, as to who was responsible for the mess, they devised a wicked plan.

It was on the night of the new moon, the night when fairy shadows are at their weakest, that the warlock planned to capture a sleeping fairy. Cackling with mischief, Tasha made a moon brew and dribbled magic words into it. As her potion boiled, its steam rose high into the sky and wrapped itself around the moon. There it adhered the moon to the sky for much longer than nature allowed. By breaking the moon's rhythm, Tasha bewitched all fairy shadows into deep slumber.

It was then that her husband set to wandering through the night in search of a fairy. At last, he came upon a fairy dusted sunflower. There inside, lay a sleeping fairy boy and his shadow.

"Ha, how easy this is," said Thames. He placed the boy inside his pocket and went home. When the moon magic ceased, the boy awoke.

"Where am I," said the fairy, "and where is my shadow?"

He stood up and was surprised to find that he was not in his forest home, but inside a house. "It is forbidden for me to enter a house. Who brought me here?" he said.

From the dark, a voice said, "I brought you here, fairy boy. I have trapped you within these walls and you cannot escape."

"I will!" said the fairy.

"No, you can never leave, for don't you see, you have lost your shadow? You know a fairy is never free without his shadow."

The fairy tried to escape, but his strength waned. When he heard a cackling laugh, he shivered. "Who's that?"

"It's I, Witch Tasha. You'd better get used to taking orders, because you'll be working for us until your life runs out."

Meanwhile, beneath a late rising sun, Shadow awakened to find his fairy gone. He searched for many months, and so it happened that one day he came to the warlock's house. Upon looking in, he saw his fairy beneath the table sweeping crumbs. "Oh, how pale and weak he seems. If only I could attach myself to him," thought Shadow, "then, we would be free to fly away."

However, the dark house made Shadow cautious. "This is an evil house," he said. "What if I fall asleep once again perhaps, this time, never to awaken." At this, he trembled.

The boy, sensing Shadow's tremble, drew towards the darkened window. Staring through a crack in the paint, he said, "Shadow!"

Upon hearing his shout, Tasha laughed. "Remember you cannot escape. Try as you might, you cannot go out, and your shadow cannot come in." This was true.

Day after day shadow flew around the house. Rescue seemed hopeless, until one bright day when he decided to ask Sun for help. He flew up and up until, he reached the sun.

"What is it that you need from me?" said Sun.

"Oh Sun, please help me free my fairy from Warlock Thames and Witch Tasha. If I can enter the warlock's house, I will be able to free my fairy. However, to do this I need your sunlight."

"That can't be done," said Sun.

"I just need a tiny drop."

"What you need is a teardrop of sunlight, but first you must make me cry, and that is impossible. I never cry."

Nevertheless, Shadow tried. He made up sad stories of bully clouds that blocked Sun's light, but Sun laughed. At last, a resigned Shadow told Sun of his fairy, and the joy they had playing in sunlight. Shadow told of the warlock's evil plan. He told how the witch's spell held up the new moon for much too long, and he told of how he missed his fairy.

Sun grew sad and squinted. He squinted long and hard until a tiny sundrop fell from his eye. Shadow caught it and thanked Sun.

When he got to Thames' house, Shadow rolled himself tightly around the sundrop and flew down the chimney into the house. The darkness held no power over Shadow now for he possessed the power of sunlight. Shadow unrolled himself and set the sundrop before the boy. Awakened, the fairy boy sat up to find his shadow in the midst of flames.

A shout arose from the warlock. "Fire? What's going on?" Seeing Shadow, Thames yelled to Tasha, "Quickly, put a spell on that shadow!" But, much to their dismay, Shadow attached himself to his fairy and escaped to Fairyland.

Faery Pond
by C. S. Frye

Awakened when a dew drop
Splattered on my head,
I jumped from the lily bulb
Where I made my bed.

I dried my face with a petal
And slid down a stem.
It was nearly midnight.
The show would soon begin.

I must hurry to the clearing,
Near the rushes green.
For on this special night,
We'll choose the Summer Queen.

The grass was cold and slippery,
As I ran across the field.
I wanted to get there early,
In that secret place concealed.

The special pond was hidden

From unbelieving eyes.
Its magic would be on display,
After the full moon rise.

Faery dust and fireflies,
Dazzle the shadowed night.
The Faeries' glistening wings,
Made a bedazzling sight.

I squatted on a grapevine,
Above the beautiful scene.
With all my friends around me,
And me, huddled in between.

The booming trumpet sounded.
A new faery sauntered out.
Dressed in snow-white feathers,
She bowed and danced about.

Her hair shined like cornsilk.
She wore a violet wreath.
After her dance, she bowed once more
Amid the fresh spring heath.

A hush filled the forest,
As the Queen received her crown.
Then I jumped from my grapevine,
And all the faeries danced around.

Teapot Tales

About the Authors

C.S. Frye (Sue) is a children's author from Ohio, North Carolina, and she presently resides in West Virginia. Sue also sings in a band, dances and writes poetry. You can visit her here: http://www.inkler.blogspot.com

*****

Kelly McDonald has been entertaining with stories and magic for more than 15 years as the Magical Faerie Crystall. She is married with 2 beautiful children and spends as much time on her writing and art as possible. She has been involved in many challenges and groups, including 12x12, chapter book challenge and WOWnonfiction. Kelly has been awarded a first and third in the Australian CYA conference, and has numerous Commended and Highly Commended awards for her writing. Her fantasy art can be found at www.facebook.com/gardenbabies or www.gardenbabyfaeries.webs.com and her author page is www.facebook.com/kelly.mcd.author.illustrator.

*****

Rebecca Fyfe, an author with stories in several anthologies and collections, is a mother of seven children and, having lost over 145 lbs. of excess weight, blogs about health and fitness at www.skinnydreaming.com. Because of her love for reading, she graduated with a degree in English Literature. She is a Californian who married an Englishman and now resides in Great Britain. Rebecca created and runs the Chapter Book Challenge which runs every March, and, when not writing short stories or children's stories, she's busy creating urban fantasy novels, full of her own special blend of magic. She gets her inspiration from her five daughters and two sons. She is the founder of Melusine Muse Press and owns several on-line gift shops, one of which can be found at www.moondusters.com. You can find her on Facebook at www.facebook.com/rebeccafyfe, Twitter at www.twitter.com/moonduster and through her author blog at http://rebeccafyfe.blogspot.com .

*****

Brenda A. Harris is a Texas author, illustrator, teacher and natural storyteller. She homeschooled her four children and influenced their passion for writing, reading, and the arts. Now a teacher, Brenda uses stories to stimulate imagination. Her students learn the joy of creating, publishing and storytelling. Brenda believes good stories help children become strong readers and writers. To learn more about Brenda go to: www.drawacircle.net.

*****

Melissa Gijsbers is an Australian based children's author and blogger. When not writing and coming up with new ideas for stories, she is running around after two active boys and working in the family business. As well as the Chapter Book Challenge, she is also part of the 12x12 picture book challenge and is a member of the SCBWI. You can find out more at www.melissagijsbers.com.

*****

Jackie Castle graduated from UT Southwestern Medical Center of Dallas. She is a published freelance writer, storyteller and elementary educator. She lives in Texas with her husband, two teenagers, and her dog, Ginger (aka ginger-roonie). When she's not teaching, she is traipsing through the worlds of Alburnium or Fae in search of another story. You can find her books on her Amazon author page at http://www.amazon.com/Jackie-Castle/e/B00AJMCRV4/ref=ntt_athr_dp_pel_1

*****

Nicole Zoltack writes fantasy stories for all ages. When she isn't writing about knights or zombies, she enjoys her family and riding horses (pretending they're unicorns, of course!). To learn more about Nicole and her writing, visit http://www.NicoleZoltack.com or http://NicoleZoltack.blogspot.com

*****

Ashley Howland lives in Adelaide, South Australia with her husband Ross, two daughters, Maddy and Aijay, her spoilt Labrador, Stitch. Her girls inspire her every day to write children's books and the dogs often provide the material. Ashley also works as the curriculum manager for Labs 'n Life. This requires random extra Labradors to appear in their lives and of course in Ashley's stories. You can find more information about Ashley and her books here: http://ahowland.org

*****

Melinda Lancaster is a children's author and a poet, with a piece of poetry hanging in the Hyannis JFK Museum, a member of SCBWI, The Cape Cod Writer's Center and the Cape Cod Children's Writers. She is a US Navy veteran, an avid volunteer, and single mom of three, one of whom has Rett Syndrome, with two stepdaughters and four grandchildren. She loves to read, write and help her daughter, Katelin, achieve all that is possible. Find out more about her at http://www.capecodchildrenswriters.com .

*****

Bron Rauk-Mitchell is an Aussie mum of 4 and 2 furbabies. Bron has a B/A, majoring in English and History, and has plans to further her studies in the near future. Bron tries to pack as much into life as possible, which is reflected by her many projects and interests. More about Bron's adventures can be found at: http://essentialbronmitchell.blogspot.com.au

*****

Satori Cmaylo has been an RN in the E.R. a competitive bodybuilder, a medium and the creator of The Satori System, a human energy system. This is her first published work. You can find out more at www.satorisystem.org.

*****

Elizabeth Gallagher is an artist, baker, and writer for children. She resides in a New Hampshire seaside home called Toad Cottage with her husband and two children. Beth is a longtime member of the Society of Children's Book Writers and Illustrators and a member of The SeaSprites writer's group. The foxes, toads, tree frogs, rabbits, raccoons, weasels and mountain lion that all share the grounds of Toad Cottage serve as muses for Beth' magical tales. Find out more at http://semayawitoadcottage.blogspot.com .

*****

Linda Schueler rediscovered her love of telling a story when she was living in China in 2005, writing for magazines like "Metropolis" and "City Weekend." Since coming back to Canada, she has focussed on writing both children's stories and short stories for adults. Linda had her short story "Rainbow" printed in "Inkspots" in 2011. In 2013, she was named a literary artist at The Cambridge Mayor's Celebration of the Arts. When not creating her latest story, she helps her husband with his international business (assisting with the writing, of course) or enjoys seeing life through the eyes of her energetic daughter, inspired by their experiences together. Find out more about Linda at www.lindaschueler.com.

*****

Robert Fyfe is a father of seven children and husband to Rebecca Fyfe. He works in IT Business Management, and when he finds a spot of that elusive "spare time" people so often talk about, he does a bit of writing. You can find some of his fairy photo manipulations at www.fairymagicphotos.co.uk.

*****

Julia Lela Stilchen is passionately driven by imagination and the exploration of new and original ideas for artistic expression - visually and in the art of storytelling. Her favorite genres are fantasy, futuristic and paranormal. She currently lives overseas with her husband and two children in Tokyo, Japan. Find out more about her on her website at www.julialelastilchen.com.

*****

Tia Mushka grew up in rural Ontario, Canada surrounded by trees, fireflies, and lots of frogs. She wrote and drew stories, like any kid. She especially loved drawing trees, and ever since then, they held a treasured spot in her writing and artwork. Even in university, her painting teacher told her it looked like fairies should be holding hands and dancing around in her forest! She received a Bachelor of Fine Arts from Brigham Young University, where she studied sculpture, and briefly geology. Taking those two loves, she took a trip to Pietra Santa, Italy where she learned how to carve stone. She learned to love history, pattern and storytelling. When she had her own children, she began to write again, taking inspiration from beloved fairy tales of her youth.

*****

Cecilia Clark is an Australian writer. Her short stories and flash fiction feature in a number of anthologies and ezines. She lives on the south west coast of Victoria in the lovely seaside town of Warrnambool. She has yet to develop an online presence but her children intend to change that.

*****

Theresa Nielsen, writer with many stories to tell and share with the world, lives in Michigan with her husband and a menagerie of pets.

*****

Yvonne Mes is a children's author, illustrator and SCBWI member. She writes short stories, picture books and junior novels. Yvonne grew up in Amsterdam, The Netherlands, and moved to outback Australia as a young adult, she now lives in Brisbane, Australia. Her background in children's services and visual arts has led to many years of sharing creativity with children of all ages and many cultures. Her three sons make sure she is never lost for an adventure or inspiration. She loves life, learning and creative challenges. You can find out more about Yvonne Mes on her website www.yvonnemes.weebly.com.

*****

David Jamieson started writing for children when he found out he was going to be a grand-dad for the 1st time and he has never looked back. He wrote "The Mansion at the Bottom of the Garden" for his granddaughter Alisha, and then went onto to write for his niece, nephews and his 2nd grandchild. He is currently working on "Beware What You Wish For" about a troll and peasant girl and "Dr Gnu," part of his Lionel Mane series written for older children. You can find his work on http://twomindsltd.webs.com.

*****

Angelica Fyfe is an aspiring scientist, currently at University, learning all she can about animals, life, and science. In her spare time, she has accumulated an odd assortment of interests which have become her passions, including parkour, ninjutsu, belly-dance and, of course, creative writing. She is also a bit of a know-it-all when it comes to myths, magic, and monsters, and knows way too much about signs and symbols for her field of study (*mitsudomoe, anyone?*). If you can think of anyone more suited to fall through a fairy-hole, she'd love to meet them!

*****

Editor: Rebecca Fyfe
Assistant Editors:
Scott Hunter
Victoria Boulton

Cover art by:
Kelly McDonald

Inside art by:
Brenda A. Harris
Cecilia Clark
Robert Fyfe

The Chapter Book Challenge

This anthology is a work created by members of the Chapter Book Challenge.

The Chapter Book Challenge, otherwise known as ChaBooCha, was created by Rebecca Fyfe and first ran in 2012. It runs every year in the month of March. The challenge is to write one completed first draft of an early reader, chapter book, middle grade book or YA novel in the month of March, starting on the 1st of March and finishing on the 31st of March.

During the month of March, there are helpful blog posts from published authors, agents and publishers to help members hone their craft, and there are prizes available throughout the challenge.

ChaBooCha has a very relaxed atmosphere where members help each other to achieve writing goals. You can sign up on the website at www.chaboocha.com, and you can also join the Facebook page for updates and information at www.facebook.com/chapterbookchallenge. There is a Twitter page at www.twitter.com/ChaBooCha1 and members interact with one another throughout the year in the Facebook group at www.facebook.com/groups/chapterbookchallenge.

It is completely free to join the Chapter Book Challenge. Proceeds from the sale of this anthology go towards the costs of running ChaBooCha.

Made in the USA
Lexington, KY
06 October 2015